Notice Me

"I'm completely and utterly in love with Scott Lawes, but it's like I don't exist to him. How can you make a boy fall for you? I have a plan, but it involves asking his best friend to help me. I'll do whatever I have to if it means getting Scott to notice me."

Jenny wants Scott, and ropes Nick into her plans to get Scott to really see her as a girl he could date.

Before Nick knows what's happening he's falling for the girl that wants his best friend. Can he make her notice him instead before it's too late?

A new young adult romantic comedy, from the acclaimed author of The Flirting Games Series

Books by Stella Wilkinson

The Flirting Games (Book One)
More Flirting Games (Book Two)
Further Flirting Games (Book Three)
The Flirting Games Trilogy, (Books 1 - 3)
Good @ Games (Book Four)
Flirting with Friends (Book Five)
Best Frenemies (Book Six)
Boy Girl Games (Book Seven)
A Compass Court Christmas (Book Eight)
Magic & Mayhem (Books 1 - 3)
Halloween Magic & Mayhem (Book One)
Werewolf Magic & Mayhem (Book Two)
Solstice Magic & Mayhem (Book Three)
Demon Magic & Mayhem (Book Four)
Notice Me
Remind Me
A Christmas Gift
The Fake Valentine
A Summer Thing
All Hallows Eve
Four Seasons of Romance

If you would like to be informed immediately when future books by this author are released then visit the website www.stellawilkinson.com

Notice Me

by
Stella Wilkinson

For Hannah
For the priceless and hilarious memories
herein

Contents

Part 1 – Jenny

Stella Wilkinson

Noticing Him

How do you make a boy notice you?

I've had a crush on Scott Lawes for months now, and if I hoped it was a passing phase, then I was wrong. It keeps getting stronger. He's just *so* gorgeous.

He's got blond hair that flops right into his eyes, a killer smile, big baby blues, and a great body. He's very sporty, in fact he's vice-captain of most of the school teams.

Not the captain; I didn't fall for the super jock. That would be Damon West. Damon is captain of *everything*, and Damon is the muscle-bound heartthrob of Blue River School. And I didn't fall for the resident bad boy. That would be Nick Weathergale, the dark sexy one that tons of girls sigh over, the love-'em-and-leave-'em flirt.

No, I fell for the funny one. The joker of the pack. The one who lights up a room, who makes me smile even when it's pouring with rain and I don't have an umbrella, the one everybody likes no matter who they are. Funny is sexy.

Add gorgeous to funny and it's pretty lethal. Well, it is for me.

I've known Scott since we were eleven, but it wasn't until my seventeenth birthday that I finally realized a veritable God had been living amongst us.

For my seventeenth I went out for pizza with a large crowd of friends. They weren't all out for me. There are three of us with our birthdays in the same week, so we decided to combine a pizza party on the Saturday night to celebrate.

I think it was Becky who invited Scott. But it could have been anyone really; it wasn't an invitation-only kind of party. About forty friends and casual acquaintances from my school were there and it was all going great. Right up until the moment I stepped outside for some air and found my boyfriend kissing a girl I used to call my friend.

I'd been dating Will for about three months. It wasn't love, but it had been nice. We'd flirted on and off for about a month and then he'd asked me out. Simple as that. I was thrilled because he was my first "official" boyfriend. We held hands, we kissed, he carried things for me and he bought me a pair of earrings. All was going well, in my opinion, right up until I found him wrapped around Carrie Grey. *Carrie Grey The Easy Lay*, that's what my friends call her (at least they do now). Maybe things with me just hadn't been moving fast enough for Will? I don't know. I thought we were both in the same place in the relationship. But I heard on the grapevine that a week after I dumped him he was bragging that Carrie had put out already and how satisfied he was, so I guess that's all he really wanted.

Anyway, finding them together on my seventeenth kind of put a downer on my night. Yeah, I may have gotten way more upset than the scumbag deserved. But at the time it felt like a punch in the gut. I think I actually burst into tears and ran off. It irritates me now that I let him even see that I was hurt, but it was my special day! He could have at least cheated on me on a regular day, instead of crapping on my birthday.

I went round the side of the building into the shadows and had a good cry. Then I texted Andrea, my best friend, and asked her to bring out my bag. My face was a mascara-streaked mess, and I couldn't go back inside looking that way.

I was kicking the wall just for the hell of it when I heard a voice say, "Who's that?"

At first I was terrified. I was in a dark alley on my own, but then I recognized Scott's golden hair in the light from the street and sighed with relief.

"It's me, Jenny." I told him, staying in the shadows.

"What are you doing out here?" He moved closer.

"Um. Kicking the wall in the balls?" I sniffed, trying to hide my tears.

He laughed, "Why?"

"Well, it's the wall or Will Dobright. He's out front swapping spit with Carrie Grey. But he's supposed to be here with me."

"Oh, I see." He ducked into the alley with me and leaned against the wall. "I wouldn't bother taking it out on the wall. He'll get his comeuppance. Paul shagged her last week and now he's got crabs."

I burst out laughing. I didn't know if he was serious or not, but it cheered me up no end.

"Anyway, they're not outside now, so you can stop hiding down here. Plus I think someone might have peed against this wall." He wrinkled his nose at the alley smell and hastily moved away from the wall. "It wasn't you, was it?" There was a twinkle in his eyes as he said it and I knew he was joking, but I glared at him anyway for even suggesting I would do such a thing!

"I can't go back in there," I said. "Everyone will know about Will and Carrie by now, plus I look like a mess."

"Don't be silly, you look as lovely as always." He gave me an adorable half smile and my heart did a funny flip-flop.

It was only one of many many funny flip-flops that my heart would do around this boy in the months to come, but I particularly remember it because it was the first one.

He thought I always looked lovely?

I smiled back, feeling a little better, and stepped out of the shadows.

"Uh oh!" Scott stopped me, and tipped my chin up to get a better look at my face. "Scratch that last comment. You *are* a mess."

"Argh! I knew it!" I hid my face in my hands. "Where the sodding bells is Andrea with my bag?"

"I'm over here." She appeared at the corner. "Sorry, Jen. I couldn't find it for ages. It was under a pile of coats. Hi, Scott." She did a shoulder hunch and blinked fast, which she thinks is cute, and gave away the fact she thought Scott was worthy of it.

I gave her a small smile, and then fished in the bag until I came up with a mirror and a tissue, and attempted to wipe my face. I had black streaks down my cheeks and I looked minging. There was no way I was going back through the crowd to get to the bathroom for a real repair job.

"It doesn't matter; thanks anyway, Andi. But it's nearly eleven and I just want to go home."

"You can't leave," she said, horrified. "It's your birthday, there's a cake."

"I'm sorry. I not in the mood anymore." I shook my head decisively.

"But… my dad's not picking us up for another hour, and you can't walk home on your own. Shall I wait with you for a taxi?"

"I'll walk you," Scott said as I opened my mouth to argue. "I have an early swim meet, so I was heading home anyway. You live right off King Street don't you? It's on my way."

Andrea began to nod at me like a mad head-bobbing thing you get in a car window, and gave Scott another barrage of eye-blinking. "That would be *so* kind, Scott. Text me when you get home, Jen?"

"Are you sure?" I asked Scott as Andrea hurried back into the pizza place. "I didn't know you live near me."

"A bit further on," Scott said, checking the street before steering me out of the alleyway. "I back onto the river near the old bridge."

"Oh, okay, great. Thanks."

"Are you sure you're going to be able to make it up Lords Hill in those heels?" His eyes travelled down from my skirt to my feet and back up again in a lazy manner. Was he checking me out? Surely not. I wasn't his type. I was too quiet and wallflower-like to attract his attention. I mean, sure, we knew each other; we were in the same form and several classes together at school. But even though I was often hanging out at the same places that he was, and we had some mutual friends, our groups didn't overlap much.

I looked down at the heels in question. It was true that they weren't my usual style, but it was supposed to be a special night and I had dressed up. To be honest, I had my doubts about getting all the way home without hobbling, but I suddenly wanted nothing more than a long walk with Scott Lawes, and a few blisters would be worth it.

"I'll be fine. I often go out in heels." I didn't feel bad about stretching the truth; after all, it was going to hurt me a lot more than him by the time we got back to my place.

We dawdled up the hill, enjoying the late June night. Conversation was a bit awkward at first. Mostly we just talked about films. I hadn't seen half of them, but I enjoyed listening to him describing the details he liked. He kept doing comedy one-liners in the voice of the actors who said them. I don't know why but I found it sexy.

I think being really good at something should be considered a major factor in attraction. I liked the way he was excellent at sport and I really liked that he was a talented mimic. Most of all I liked that he made me laugh. How could I not have noticed before that he was all that, as well as really easy on the eye?

If it hadn't been for my aching feet, then I would have sworn we had barely left the pizza place before we were on my road.

We had got there too fast. I wanted to stretch the night on and on. I wasn't ready to say goodbye just yet.

I sat down on the wall outside my house and winced as I eased my shoes off a bit. Thankfully he didn't seem to notice.

I patted the wall next to me. Scott glanced at his watch and then shrugged and sat down.

"So what's the story with you and Stacey?" I said. It was cheeky to ask, but after half an hour of walking and talking together, I felt we were comfortable enough to get a bit more personal in our conversation.

"We broke up last week. She wanted more of my time and I have too many commitments already. She was kind of whiny, and she wanted me to give up swimming."

I silently shook my head at her stupidity. If Scott were my boyfriend there's no way I would nag him to give up swimming. He clearly loved it more than he had loved any girl.

"I can just imagine how she would have acted when cricket season started." I joked, trying to show him I understood.

He raised his eyebrows at me; hopefully he was impressed that I remembered he was on the cricket team and how time-consuming that was during the summer. Maybe he didn't know that half the girls in our school kept their noses pressed to the window when the cricket squad came out on the field.

There was something about those tight, white, bum-hugging... I stopped thinking about it.

"So do you think you might forgive Dobright? Or should I call him Not-so-bright?" Scott asked in return.

"No chance." I shook my head.

"Good." Scott gave me that adorable smile again, the one with just one corner turned up, and my heart flip-flopped once more.

"I'd better be off." He stood up and I shot to my feet as well, ignoring the cries of my heels. I desperately tried to think of a way to make him stay longer but came up with nothing.

I stared into his eyes. I wasn't under any illusion that this was special for him. He'd just been dropping me off on his way home, but I wanted to somehow convey that it had been special for me. That things like this didn't happen to me often.

I tried to give him a "speaking look", but my eyes must have been on mute because he didn't seem to get it.

He tilted his head like a question, and when I stood there and didn't say anything, he lowered his face to mine.

Then he kissed me.

Even though I had been willing him to do it for at least the last twenty minutes, it was still a shock.

Okay, it wasn't a real kiss. Unfortunately. There were no open mouths or tongues in the kiss; it was just a gentle brushing of his lips against mine. But a zing shot straight from my lips to my stomach and then bounced about in there, making me feel totally over excited.

It was over in a heartbeat, and I had to wonder for a second if it had even happened or if I had imagined it.

"Happy birthday, Jenny." Scott pushed up from the wall and I knew the moment was over.

"Thanks for walking me home." I tried to sound

casual.

"No problem. Anytime." He gave me a little wave and then sauntered off down the road.

I stood and watched until he turned the corner, wondering if he'd look back, but he didn't.

I went into my house on a total high. My parents were in bed so I sneaked up the stairs and into my room, trying not to dance all the way.

Then I clutched my giant teddy bear to my face and squealed into his fur for a full minute until I'd gotten it out.

Then I texted Andrea: "Home safe. OMG Scott sort of kissed me!"

Her reply was instant, "WHAT??? You lucky cow. W' U mean by sort of?"

I had to think about that. How did I describe the almost kiss? On paper it was the sort of kiss he might give his mother; except it had been on the lips, and I wasn't family. So what had it meant? Something or nothing? I didn't know...

I needed to talk to Andrea in person, but I was

bound to wake my parents if I started talking on the phone and she might still be out.

"I'll tell you L8r, gotta sleep now. XX"

I lay in bed and relived every word we'd said, over and over. How was it possible to go straight from being one person's girlfriend, to totally over them, and obsessing about another guy, in just a few short hours?

I'd always known Scott was gorgeous and funny, but how had I not been a gibbering mess around him for years? Why had I only tonight noticed he was the most amazing guy ever?

I didn't have the answers, but I was fairly sure this was the beginning of something. He'd walked me home and he'd kinda kissed me.

So where did we stand now? Was he going to make us official? Had I truly caught the interest of Super Hot Scott? (My new name for him).

I went through Sunday in a daze; I couldn't wait for school on Monday. I checked my phone repeatedly, wondering if he might call or text for a date, but he didn't. I bent Andrea's ear for about two hours on the subject and she agreed he was obviously into me and clearly wonderful.

I got up at silly o'clock to get ready for school, all full of adrenaline at the thought of seeing Scott again. I actually ditched my trainers for cork wedges, and my usual school jeans were replaced by my tight "going-out" jeans. I spent almost an extra hour on my minimal makeup, and I tried on about thirty different tops before settling on the coral halter with matching shrug.

I walked in to registration feeling like I was floating on air. Life was about to get fantastic.

There was Scott, at his usual desk, sitting with his chair turned around backwards as he chatted to his friends.

He looked up as I entered and I gave him a huge smile and a wave, "Hi!"

He didn't say anything, just gave me a nice smile and a nod as if to acknowledge my presence and then turned back to his friends.

I stopped dead.

That was pretty much identical to how he'd always treated me. Not as though I didn't exist, but as though I was a casual acquaintance.

Someone bumped into my back, forcing me forward, and I stumbled to my desk in confusion.

I think my face was actually dumbstruck in the "Huh?" position.

Hadn't we bonded on our walk home? Hadn't we shared a magical moment? Hadn't he sort of kissed me and totally rocked my little world?

Hadn't it meant *anything* to him?

Well, obviously not.

At first I thought maybe he was playing it cool. Like he didn't want to lose face in front of his friends, or maybe it was too soon after breaking up with Stacey. But as the days turned into a week, and then two, I had to face the fact that all that had happened was that I had totally and utterly fallen for him, and he didn't feel anything at all!

And so began my unrequited adoration of Scott Lawes. My first serious crush.

But I didn't want to just adore him from afar, I wanted this boy to be mine! I wanted him to fall madly in love with me and we'd live happily ever after.

I had to find a way to *make* him notice me. And boy, did I have a plan...

Getting Help

"I have a plan to make Scott Lawes notice me, but I need your help."

Andrea screwed her face up at my words.

"Why do I get the feeling I'm not going to like this?" She gave me a nudge and I automatically nudged her back.

"Please, Andi. You know I'd do it for you." I gave her my best puppy-dog eyes.

She narrowed her own eyes at me. "What exactly would you do for me?"

I took a deep breath. "Well... The problem, as I see it, is that as far as Scott is concerned I don't really exist."

She nodded cautiously, encouraging me to continue.

"So basically he needs to see a lot more of me."

"Let me guess – you're planning to take up sports?" Her voice was full of amused disbelief.

"Don't laugh," I chided. "This is important to me. But no, nothing as dramatic as that! I've written a list of things he does, places he goes, and who his friends are."

I dug out my notepad and a pen.

"So you're planning on stalking him?" She was still teasing, but I was deadly serious.

"Uh, yes, actually. I want to be everywhere he is until he realizes what a lot we have in common, and that's kind of where you come in."

"Uh oh." She mimed a psycho knife attack. "What exactly am I supposed to do? Follow him around with a walkie-talkie feeding back his movements when you're not there?"

"Even better." I gave her a big smile. "You're going to date Fat Brad and he's going to tell you."

She choked on her drink. When she stopped coughing, "I'm going to what?" she squeaked.

"Listen," I said, jabbing my pen in her direction, "Scott goes out with his friends a lot, right? And we don't get invited because we're not in his group. So how do we get into his group? One of us has to get chummy with one of his friends." I smiled as if it were simple.

"No way! Not on your life, Jen. When have I ever asked you to do anything like that for me?"

"Hmm, how about the time you threw up on the back of Danny Cannon's head on the school bus and I pretended it was me because you had a crush on him? Or the time you sat in dog crap and I gave you my skirt and wore my gym kit for a whole day because you were supposed to be meeting Brandon Snider for lunch? Or..."

"Okay, okay, I owe you! But *Fat Brad?*"

"I know," I sighed, "but he's the obvious choice. He's liked you since we were about five years old, and he isn't actually fat any more, is he? He lost all that weight last year; it's just a nickname now. And he's not *bad*-looking. I'm not suggesting you actually have to date him, but maybe you could flirt with him a bit? Give off the impression that you *might* be interested, if only you hung out more? Then perhaps casually ask what he's up to for the weekend or where they might all be going?"

Andrea rolled her eyes. "So I'm to be the sacrificial lamb to the slaughter? Great! If I do this, we are *so* even, got it?"

I grinned and hugged her. I'd known she would do it in the end, but I thought I was going to have to beg a lot harder.

"Humph. So what will you be doing while I'm destroying my rep?" she said.

"What rep? Face it, Andi, we're invisible at this school. If anything, this will boost your rep. And don't worry, you won't be the only one putting yourself out there. I'm going to turn the charm on Nick Weathergale and try to get him to dish all Scott's personal deets. After all, Nick is Scott's best mate after Damon."

"Really, how will you manage that without being obvious?" Andrea looked sceptical.

"You're not the only one who owes me. You know Nick is my lab partner in Science? Well, I'm pretty much carrying him right now. Plus he's really nice, he doesn't act like I'm invisible, so if I have to then I might even just tell him the truth."

She shook her head at me. "That's certainly putting yourself out there. I see this ending in a truckload of embarrassment! I wouldn't trust Nicholas Weathergale as far as I could throw him. He's a tart and he'll eat you for breakfast. He'd probably get a kick out of humiliating you. Plus isn't he going out with Alice Chan? She'll rearrange your face if you try to 'charm' him. Is Scott really worth all this?"

"Well, aren't you a ray of sunshine in the mornings? Yes, Scott is totally worth it, and no, I don't think Nick will use it to humiliate me. After all, his grade depends on me doing all the work while he sits around looking too cool for school. And as for Alice, well, she probably won't last the month, none of his girlfriends do."

Andrea shrugged at me. "It's your funeral. Just remember that you will probably be taking me down with you."

I gave her another nudge, "In that case we can be bottom-feeders together. *None shall pass*! Right?"

She gave me a hefty shove back, but smiled and said, "Nerd."

We both looked up as Fat Brad walked past.

Andrea sighed, "I've got a Geography lesson with him right now." She crumpled her juice carton and stood up.

"Go, girl. Take one for the team," I teased.

"Fine. But *the team* owes me an ice cream after school!"

Ten minutes later I was sitting in Chemistry, watching Nick out of the corner of my eye and wondering how to broach the subject of Scott.

Nick was Scott's opposite. He was dark and lean. His face reminded me of some kind of bird of prey. His hooded eyes were deceptive; he saw everything.

"Spit it out, Jones," he said, not even looking away from his notebook.

I jumped. "Spit what out?"

"Whatever it is you're thinking of asking me." He glanced up and I swallowed. How did he do that? How did he always know?

"Uh, I was just wondering what you were up to this weekend?" I said, lamely.

Nick leaned back and gave me an appraising once-over.

"Stop it." I flicked my pen at him.

"What?" he said innocently.

"Stop acting like I said something crude!" I huffed.

"Jones. You insult me. I'm merely curious about this sudden interest in my plans and whether you might finally have started appreciating the perfection that sits beside you?"

"Oh, get over yourself. You know I have zero interest in your massive over inflated ego! Just forget it." I turned back to the petri dish in front of us, feigning intense interest in the agar I found there.

"Sorry, go on – what is you really want to know? That I was thinking of watching the 'Supernatural' marathon on TV this weekend? Or that I'm hanging with friends at The Coach House Saturday night? Or that I'm playing five-a-side on Sunday morning? Which bit of that might be worthy of discussion to you?"

I swallowed again. "The Coach House?" I said tentatively, waiting for him to start teasing me.

He sat up straighter. "You want to come?"

The Coach House was an old building where local bands played on the weekends, sort of a showcase of new talent. I'd never been, but a lot of people from school talked about it.

I sighed, I'd known it was going to be impossible to play it cool with Nick; he was too smart in the ways of the female mind to miss the obvious.

"Are you inviting me?" I asked flippantly.

"Like a date?" Nick frowned at me.

"No. Not like a date! I just... thought I should get out there a bit more, you know? Mingle."

Nick smiled and leaned back again. "Who is he?"

"I don't know what you're talking about." I bent towards the petri dish again, my nose practically touching the disgusting jelly inside.

"Come on, Jones. You can tell me. You're obviously not hankering for *my* bod or you would have gone with the 'Supernatural' marathon. Who do you really want to see more of?"

I chewed on my bottom lip, like I always do when I'm nervous. Time for plan B.

"I might have a tiny crush on Scott," I said almost as a whisper.

Nick threw back his head and laughed, exactly as I knew he would; and I turned beet red.

I waited patiently for him to finish laughing. It wasn't *that* funny.

"Have you tried just telling him?" Nick eventually calmed down enough to say.

I gave him an "As if!" look.

Nick shrugged. "Scott isn't that scary. He doesn't have girls queuing round the block, well, not masses; he might be flattered."

"No," I said firmly, "I just can't. It would be too embarrassing. Right now I just want him to notice me. And if you want to pass Chemistry, you have to promise to keep your mouth shut, okay?"

He held up his hands. "Whatever you say, Jones."

He paused for a long moment before adding in a more serious tone, "Of course you're invited on Saturday night. Bring Andrea. The band will probably be lame, but we'll have fun anyway."

We were quiet for a few minutes while I glowed with success and tried to concentrate on the science problem on the board, but really I was thinking how easy that had been. Was it really that simple to get a social life? Just ask someone what they were doing and wait to be invited?

Nick broke the silence. "He doesn't see you as a girl, you know."

"What?" My head jerked up.

"You're too sweet. Like someone's little sister. You need to start by making him aware that you're all grown up now."

I bit my lip again. I wasn't actually sure if I was *all grown up*. But I was willing to take any advice being offered.

"How?" I said.

Nick very deliberately checked me out again. I

crossed my arms over my chest as his gaze lingered too long on my assets.

"Do you own any outfits that are a bit less conservative? It will be a night out, can you sex it up a bit?"

"Scott isn't like that." I said defensively.

Nick laughed at me again. "We're all like that, honey-pie, it's how we're built."

I thought about it for a couple of minutes. What would it hurt to show a little more flesh, if it made Scott realize I was a girl – a girl he might want to date?

"Yeah, I can do that," I confirmed.

Nick gave me a nod of approval and I felt excited inside. The plan was coming together. This Saturday I was going to work it, and Scott *was* going to notice me.

Bad Odds

I put so much time and effort into getting ready for going to The Coach House that Andrea and I got there pretty late. In fact it was almost nine o'clock. I kept telling her we were fashionably late, but the words died in my mouth when the first person I saw was Scott and he was already kissing someone else!

He was sitting at a table of people from our school, but the girl in his lap was a stranger to me. A skanky stranger.

She had long, dark hair with cyan streaks at the front (which I envied), a totally transparent vest, which you could see her push-up through, and leather trousers. I mean, leather, really? She was *so* not Scott's usual type. She was also sporting a vibrant dragon tattoo on one shoulder. Did that mean she was eighteen already?

Okay, I might have been a bit biased when I called her skanky. But my mum would have had a fit if I'd even tried to leave the house like that.

I felt a rush of panic. I was totally out of my element. The lighting was too low, the music was too loud, and I only knew a few people here – and most of them I only knew on sight; they weren't actually my friends or anything.

Andrea pushed a hard finger into my back, as if she knew I was about to bolt. But how could I go over to Scott's table when he was already making out with someone else?

Then Nick raised his hand to beckon us over and a huge wave of relief swept over me.

Nick would look after us. He wouldn't let anyone scary near me. And he was giving us the all-important "in" with the group. Even if it was all too late.

I was so pleased to see his welcoming face that I gave him an impromptu kiss on the cheek, but he turned his head at the last second and I got a lip smacker instead.

I think I blushed right down to the ends of my hair, but Nick just laughed. I wasn't sure if he'd done it on purpose or not.

Andrea narrowed her eyes on him, but then Fat Brad waved from the other end of the table and she pulled a fake grimace at me before going over to say hello.

Nick pulled me down to sit next to him and I squeezed onto the bench between him and Damon (the uber-jock) feeling kind of self-conscious. Surely this was the most desirable spot in the room to sit in? I just hoped I wasn't going to get any jealous girlfriends lamping me for sitting next to either Nick or Damon, because I certainly hadn't planned it.

My heart was thumping, because it just wasn't *me* to be here with this "it" crowd. Usually by now I would be watching TV with my parents and wondering what book to take to bed.

I looked at Nick with a "help!" expression in my eyes and he smiled kindly. Leaning forward, he whispered right in my ear, "Don't worry, you look the part." Then he had the daring to actually put one finger down the front of my top!

"Sorry," he said, removing his finger, "I was just

retrieving my eyeballs from your cleavage."

I burst out laughing. "Nicholas Weathergale! Please tell me you did *not* just use the cheesiest pickup line ever on me?"

"You think that's cheesy? I have a whole bunch of them," he teased, and I realized he had done it to try to make me laugh and relax.

"What's the worst one you've ever used that actually worked?" I asked with a grin.

Nick thought for a minute. "I once told a girl that there was a party in my pants, and she was the only one invited. I'm pretty sure I got lucky that night. Although, I believe I actually went home with both her and her best friend, so if you think about it, she wasn't the only one invited after all..."

"You did not!" I was wide-eyed with shock.

"You're so gullible, Jones." Nick patted me on the knee and smirked.

"But did you really?" I had to ask.

"You'll never know." He winked at me and then signalled for a waitress. Despite how busy the place was, a girl appeared in seconds.

"A beer for me, please. What will you have, Jones? A lager top? Or maybe a cider?"

I gave him a leg pinch under the table. I was trying to point out that I wasn't old enough to drink and that I didn't have any identification if asked, but Nick put his hand over mine and pinched me back.

"A half of cider then. Thanks." He smiled at the waitress and she disappeared; just like that, no questions asked.

I gave him an unsure smile, and then, as if drawn by a magnet, my eyes went back to Scott and the skank on the other side of the table.

Thankfully they weren't sitting directly opposite me, and if I kept talking to Nick then they were out of my direct line of sight. But I was very aware of them.

"Just have a drink or two and it won't seem such a big deal," Nick said.

I pouted at him to show that it was a big deal, but he just laughed.

"It's just a kiss, Jones, not an engagement. By next

week it could be you instead."

My heart leaped at the thought, but then I picked up on the subtle warning. I thought maybe he was telling me not to be one of those girls? I chewed my lip. I didn't just want to be a hook-up, I wanted to be a girlfriend, but how did you get to be one without first being the other? Did I have to play it really cool until he was in love with me? That didn't seem very likely to happen. And would I turn him down if a kiss was in the offing? Hardly! But I really liked him; I didn't want to mess it up by being too easy. Why were the rules so complicated? Why was it so hard these days just to like someone and be liked back?

And how on earth could I get him to notice all the effort I had gone to if he was going to stay lip-locked to someone else?

"You have to think of this like recon," Nick said, clearly reading my mind again.

"Huh?" I wasn't one hundred percent sure what he was talking about, but I knew he was talking about Scott.

"Recon — like homework, you know? Just observe what works on him and what doesn't."

I nodded enthusiastically. After all, that had kind of been my plan. I had intended to follow him around and gather useful information. So maybe tonight wouldn't be a total bust after all.

I tried to watch him without being obvious. He was running his fingers over the girl's dragon tattoo and saying something which she obviously found hilarious. I couldn't blame her for that, he *was* pretty hilarious; it was one of the things I loved most about him.

I opened my mouth to ask Nick a question, but he pre-empted me.

"Yes, Jones, it is sexy."

"What?"

"The tattoo. It's sexy. It isn't the kind of thing you want a girl to display in front of your mother, and maybe it is a tiny bit trampy, but do you really think a seventeen-year-old boy cares?"

He looked at me thoughtfully. "Perhaps you should get one."

I pulled the most outraged face I could manage. "You think I should ink my skin forever just so that Scott thinks I'm up for a good time?"

Nick laughed at me. "Don't worry. No one is going to think *you're* trampy; you're still the sweet girl right now, remember? And I only meant a temporary tattoo, not a real one! It might just make him sit up a bit and notice you, is all. That's what you want, isn't it?"

"I guess so, yes." I digested that idea. After all, I was willing to try almost anything.

Suddenly I spotted something shocking over Nick's shoulder. Andrea was full-on kissing with Fat Brad!

Nick turned to see what I was staring at with my mouth wide open.

"Everyone but you, huh?" he teased me.

I punched his arm. "I was just surprised; she said she didn't like Brad. And anyway, *you're* not with anyone tonight!"

Nick leaned forwards and whispered in my ear, "Actually Jones, I'm pretty sure that most of the people around us think I'm just about to score."

I gasped, realizing that we were sitting incredibly close. Not to mention the fact that I had accidentally kissed him on arrival, then he'd jokingly put his finger in my cleavage and now he was paying for my drink.

I shuffled back a bit on the bench and glanced again at Scott, hoping that he hadn't jumped to that conclusion. He wasn't looking at us, but had he seen anything that might make him think that Nick and I were flirting?

Nick rolled his eyes at me and dragged me close again. "Jeez, Jenny. You really don't know much about boys, do you!"

"Huh? I can guess what's on your mind, if that's what you mean." I wriggled as he pulled me too close for casual friends.

"Not me, dumbo. Him. Boys are very competitive. We want what other boys have. If someone else wants something then you begin to think about that thing. You realize you should be the one to have it. We're childish like that. If no one wants the thing, then it would never occur to us that it might be desirable."

"Am I the 'thing' in this scenario?" I asked, not a little put out.

"Yes, but it isn't just about girls. It's everything. We start by fighting over the best marbles when we're three and end up fighting over the best girls."

He took a swig from his drink.

"Let me ask you a question. If you were looking at shoes, some red ones and some blue ones, and all your friends were going crazy over the red shoes and saying they wished they could have them — wouldn't you rather get the red shoes? Instead of the blue ones that nobody noticed?"

I glared at him. "Am I the shoes now? Can I just point out that women don't just think about shoes and lipstick. We have other interests."

"Yes, I know, you like boys as well." Nick pushed my drink into my hand. "Oh, calm down, Jones, I was just trying to make a point. It isn't important."

I sipped my cider slowly. Actually, I rather thought the point was important. Nick was trying to say that Scott might notice me more if other boys noticed me and said so.

I looked at Nick, wondering just how far I could push him to help me.

Stella Wilkinson

Pretend To Flirt With Someone Else

I had a brand new plan to get Scott to notice me, but I'd need Nick's help.

"Do you have a girlfriend?" I blurted. "Are you still seeing Alice?" I wanted to get that sorted before we continued, just in case she got wind of things and wanted to beat me up for it.

"No. And don't ask nosy questions," was all he said.

I thought on that for a while. It seemed fair enough; it was none of my business anyway.

"Nick?" I asked in my prettiest voice.

He raised one eyebrow suspiciously. "Ye-es?"

"You know what you were saying about Scott wanting me more if other boys liked me as well?"

He groaned and slapped his forehead. "How did I not see this one coming?" he muttered. "*Is* that what I was saying?" he asked innocently.

I furrowed my brow; wasn't that what he'd said?

He nudged me. "I'm just teasing you, Jones. Yes, it

is what I was implying – sort of, anyway."

"So, would you do that for me?" I wheedled.

"What *exactly* do you want me to do?" He hooked a finger down the front of my top again. "Shall I show everyone that I think that you're hot by groping you in public, maybe? Or perhaps we could just kiss for a while, or you could come sit on my lap?"

I was about to get all outraged when I realized he was still teasing me.

"It's okay," I reassured him. "You don't actually have to do any of those things. Just maybe drop it into conversation that you think I'm cute or something?"

"Oh" – he faked a blow to the chest – "shot down in flames as usual."

"Knock it off." I socked his leg good-naturedly. "I know you don't really like me, just as much as I know that you are almost *never* shot down!"

"So I don't get any kisses? Not even fake passion? Surely I should at least get to feel your boobs? Otherwise what's in it for me?"

I grinned at him again, knowing that he was still just

messing about.

"You get all my gratitude," I said sweetly, "which should be reflected in your science grade. Plus, wouldn't it work better for me if you told Scott that I was attractive but hard to get? Wouldn't that make me seem even more desirable?"

"Darn it! She's a fast learner." Nick's eyes twinkled. "No problem. I shall tell Scott that you are a true goddess. Beautiful but beyond my reach."

"Don't lay it on too thick or he won't believe a word of it," I said, looking at Nick's fake star-struck expression with caution.

"No, he won't, and neither would I, to be honest. You're going to have to give a little bit, maybe act like you're leading me on, or that we may or may not get together, just to pique his interest."

"How do I do that?" I chewed my lip as I gave it some thought.

Nick smiled. "You're doing it right now. Sitting here flirting with me."

"I'm not flirting with you!" I said.

"Really? I'm definitely getting a vibe off you." There was a pause, then he laughed at the expression on my face. "Don't worry, I'm not really. I know you only have eyes for Lawes. But at least it probably looks as though we're flirting to everyone else. That's good. And quite seriously, I do know exactly what to say to the boys to make you a hot property. You might find you are suddenly rather sought after; are you ready for that?"

"You're not going to tell them I'm up for *anything*? Or something awful like, that are you?"

He patted my arm. "No, quite the opposite. I'll make it look like I'm chasing you and you are hard to get. But you have to be careful not to look too disinterested. Right now they all think you are too young and sweet to be particularly interested in boys, so you'll have to act like you *might* be up for it, with the right boy of course. That dress is a good start."

I nodded, mentally taking notes. Nick might be a dreadful womanizer, but at least it proved that he knew women. And obviously he knew men too. His help was going to be invaluable.

I drank my drink and we watched the band for a bit. Scott and the skank had gone to dance a while ago and I found myself constantly scanning the floor for them. Was Scott a good dancer? Or did he do it as a parody to be amusing? Or were they just up against a wall somewhere getting it on?

"Do you want to dance?" Nick spoke in my ear, as the music seemed to pound louder than ever.

"Yes." I love to dance, but actually I really just wanted to know where Scott was and what he was doing.

Nick took my hand and led me through the tables to the dance floor; we pushed our way into the crowd a bit until we found a space.

We danced facing each other for a while, but it seemed awkward when everyone around us was sort of dirty dancing. I didn't want to bump and grind with him, but Nick solved it by moving behind me. He put his hands on my hips, following my movements, but left a good space between us. Even so, I still felt a spark of energy between us. He was still touching me, even though just my hips, as I danced, and he was moving in time to me. It was all a little bit too close for comfort.

I saw Scott; he was dancing with the girl, but they were just swaying on the spot, holding each other close. I nodded at them to Nick and he understood straight away. He turned me round and wrapped his arms around me. We slowly edged nearer to Scott.

Scott finally noticed us when we almost bumped into them.

He gave me his gorgeous smile. I grinned back at him. Then he raised his eyebrows at both of us, almost as a question at my being with Nick.

Nick laughed. "Not for the want of trying!" he said cryptically to Scott over the music.

Scott winked at me and said, "Keep up the good work."

I smiled, trying not to look confused.

Then *Urgh*, Scott began kissing that awful skank, and Nick twirled me away and back off the dance floor.

"What was that all about?" I asked, meaning the brief conversation on the dance floor. I hadn't really understood what it was about, but I knew Nick had.

"Just what you wanted me to do. I let Scott know I was trying to get physical with you, and that so far you were holding out. He was praising your restraint. After all, I *am* fairly hard to resist." he said, not at all humbly.

"You're a good friend. Thank you." I gave him a proper hug. "I think I've had enough for tonight. Would you be offended if I found Andrea and went home?"

"Nah, run along. I suppose I had better behave myself for the rest of the night now, or I'm the one who's going to look like a tart."

"Hah!" I laughed at the irony of the total double standard applied to boys and girls. "I think if you were seen with yet another girl tonight, it would only enhance your rep."

"Or the lads might think I was searching for someone to console my poor heart after your cruel rejection." Nick was pulling wounded faces again.

I rolled my eyes. "Whatever. I'll see you on Monday. Thanks again for inviting us tonight; I don't think it was a total bust."

"No, I don't think it was." Nick gave me a twisted smile and went back to his seat by Damon.

I went to find Andrea. She and Fat Brad were necking in a dark corner. She jumped about a mile when I tapped her on the shoulder, and looked up red-faced and guilty, although actually I think the red face was stubble burn. She had a glowing red chin! Brad was going to have to start shaving if he was going to keep kissing Andrea.

But she did also look really embarrassed. "Uh, hi, Jen. How's it going with you?" She tried for a breezy tone but totally failed.

"Hi, *Brad*," I said, emphasizing his name to draw to her attention that I found her situation funny. "Sorry, Andi, but I've had enough for tonight. Are you ready to bounce or do you want to stay for a while?"

She almost looked longingly at Brad's mouth. But

she said, "I'll come with you."

"I'll wait by the door," I said, just in case she wanted a more private goodbye with Brad.

When we left I couldn't help teasing her about the stubble burn. She groaned when she looked in a mirror. "That's going to sting in the morning," she grumbled. "You'd think he would have shaved if he expected to get lucky!"

"Maybe he didn't expect to? I mean you've hardly shown any interest in him for years, and now you suddenly stick your tongue down his throat?"

"Well, he was pretty fat for a lot of that time. But I think he's quite well-built now. It's a shame the nickname lasted so much longer than his waistline did."

"So do I have to stop calling him Fat Brad now? Shall we call him Buff Brad?" I teased.

Andrea giggled. "Maybe. But he is quite buff, isn't he? Or am I wearing beer goggles tonight? Is it awful that I think I might like him? I mean, I know you only wanted me to chat him up so you could get closer to

Scott; but it isn't so bad if I actually start seeing him, is it?"

I gave her a one-arm hug as we walked. "Of course not, Andi. That would be great. It's weird how he's become more popular than we are in this school, when we looked down on him at Rivermouth. Maybe it will even help our cred. And it would be brilliant for me, because we can both go along to things with Brad and the boys, and then I can look all left out while you snog with Brad, and then Scott can rescue me again." I smiled as I thought about it.

"What about Nick?" Andrea asked.

"Oh, he won't care, he'll probably be glad not to have me cramping his style. I can just cramp yours instead."

"That's not what I meant." She gave me a shove. "I meant you and Nick. You seemed pretty close?"

"Don't be silly! That was just part of the plan. There's nothing between Nick and me like that, and believe me, there never will be! But we're going to pretend a bit to pique Scott's interest. Nick has a theory that boys like girls that other boys like. Like red shoes over blue shoes. He explains it better than me."

"Hmmm." Andrea didn't look convinced. "I know how this story ends. You end up falling in love with Nick instead, but he's not boyfriend material."

I laughed long and hard at that idea. I didn't fancy Nick in the slightest, and I was totally devoted to Scott.

I just had to tip the odds in my favour a bit more, and soon Scott wouldn't be able to help but notice me.

Faking It

In Chemistry on Wednesday, Nick surprised me by asking me on a date. A fake date.

"So Trudy's friend is the lead guitarist of The Drains, and he's invited us all over to his place to listen to music on Saturday. If you want?"

I pulled off my goggles. "I'm sorry, Nick, I didn't understand a word of that. Who is Trudy and who are The Brains? And you don't need my permission, do you?"

Nick sighed, as though I was being dense. "Trudy is the girl Scott was with on Saturday, The *Drains* are the band we were watching, remember? And I was asking if you wanted to come along."

"Oh, I don't think Trudy would want *me* there. After all, she's with Scott. I can hardly turn up and try to get Scott to notice me right in front of her."

"Earth to Jennifer, we are going for the subtle approach, are we not? If you play it properly, then Scott should notice you and Trudy should be oblivious. I'm suggesting you come as my date. We flirt and show Scott you're in the big leagues now. I try to get further with you, but fail. Thus making you a desirable challenge."

"Will it really have that effect? Won't it just make me look like a tart for leading you on, or frigid for not following through?" I was excited by the idea, but nervous too. I tried to remind myself that this was exactly why I'd roped Nick in to help me. He was way more skilled at these games than I was.

"I think you'll come off just fine, Jones. You are already known for being a nice girl, so no one will judge you either way. Just try to look like you're warming up to at least kissing?"

"Do I really come across that immature? I went past kissing with Will."

"Yeah, but you're obviously still a virgin." Nick jumped as the test tube I was holding slipped from my fingers and smashed on the floor.

He fetched a dustpan and brush from the cupboard while I picked up the largest bits of glass.

"Sorry, Jen. Is it supposed to be a secret?" he said, when we had finally cleaned up.

I touched my warm cheeks, willing them to cool down. "What do you mean by obviously? And is it a bad thing? Just because I haven't wanted to do it with anyone yet? Scott is different." A dreamy smile came over my face at the thought of just kissing Scott.

Nick's jaw tightened. "I wouldn't let him know that if I were you. Don't you want him to want you for the right reasons?"

"Of course I do! I want him to fall in love with me first, but *you* said I had to look like I might be up for more."

"Yeah, but you can't act like you'd give it away if he asked. Otherwise he'll just ask! Why do you think he's with Trudy right now?" Nick seemed cross, though I wasn't sure why.

"Because he likes her?" I ventured.

"Grow up, Jones. It's because she humps like a rabbit." Nick smiled nastily at my shocked expression.

I turned away, feeling hurt. I hated the thought of

Scott with another girl, and I hated Nick being so flip about it.

He put his hand on my shoulder. "Sorry, Jen."

I forgave him instantly. He only called me Jen or Jennifer on the rare occasions when he was being serious. So I knew he meant it.

"So what do you suggest?" I asked.

"If a guy likes you, then of course he will wait until you're ready. Scott is a nice guy. I think he was just a bit bowled over by Trudy. She came on to him and was hard to resist, but I don't think he has any deep feelings for her. She's just a novelty. She's eighteen already, and most girls like her would be with someone even older. There aren't many who would be interested in guys our age. So Scott would have been mental to turn her down. You have to try these things when they come along. And just think how much he's probably learned from her about pleasing girls." Nick winked at me suggestively, and I knew we were back to teasing mode again.

Sincerity never lasted long on Nick.

On Saturday I made the sudden decision to buy a temporary tattoo. I didn't want something as scary and in-your-face as Trudy's dragon, but something a little more girly and me. So I got a butterfly.

I thought long and hard about my outfit. In the end I tried for casual sexy. My tight jeans went on again, teamed once more with my cork wedges, but I went with a cropped top, exposing my stomach, which was a first for me. It wasn't low-cut at all, but it was the most flesh I'd ever shown. I had to resist the urge to keep pulling it down to meet my jeans.

To help me embrace the bare stomach I put my butterfly tattoo right there, just to one side of my belly button. Who was to know it was fake? It was not as though any of them had seen my belly before. But if anyone asked, then my plan was to laugh and be honest that it was fake. I would say that Andrea and I had bought one each for fun or something like that.

I was a bit nervous that Andrea wasn't coming on the date, but Brad had other plans, and Nick said it was only a small gathering and that he couldn't turn up with two girls, despite his reputation.

I met Nick at the end of my road at eight thirty that night.

"Wow, scrubbing up nicely, Jones." His fingers brushed over the butterfly. "I like this."

"Because tattoos are sexy? It isn't real," I confessed.

"No, because it's hot on you. You look like a mixture of naughty and nice, sugar and spice. A helluva lot of guys will like that concept."

"But will Scott? He's the only one that matters," I said.

Nick rolled his eyes. "Yes, Jones, I think I can safely say that Scott will find you fairly irresistible too."

"But the tattoo isn't real. I should tell him that, right?"

"For goodness' sake, it isn't the tattoo; that doesn't matter. It's the blend of good girl with a little bit of bad girl. And you're pulling it off perfectly. Okay?"

"Thank you." I gave him my biggest smile and put my hand through his arm.

I didn't say so but I thought Nick looked pretty hot

himself. He was almost head-to-toe in his customary black. Black jeans and tight black t-shirt. The only adornment was that across his chest was a picture of a grey dove with its wings spread wide. His dark hair was slicked back, and being so close to him meant that I could see from my side view how impossibly long and dark his eyelashes were.

We chatted easily as we walked. He wasn't funny like Scott, but we debated politics on a level I hadn't thought he was capable of, and he surprised me with his grasp on the definitions of terrorism. I know that sounds like a really boring conversation, but I enjoyed it. I had thought we would end up talking about cars or something equally dull.

It was only a fifteen-minute walk, and I was almost disappointed when it was over. But then all these snakes started squirming in my stomach at the thought of Scott waiting inside. Of a whole evening in his company, even if he was there with another girl.

Nick rang the bell and then slipped his hand into the back pocket of my jeans, making me jump as he squeezed my bum.

"Are you sure you're ready to fake it as my date?" he teased, as I slapped at his hand.

"Yeah, yeah, just don't get too grabby!" I hissed. Then I plastered on a big fake smile as the door opened.

Eye Contact

I didn't know the guy who opened the door, but I assumed he was from the band that Nick had mentioned.

"Hi, Blake," Nick said, "This is Jennifer."

Blake gave me a rather sexual once-over, which I found uncomfortable. I was used to it from Nick, but only because I always knew he was joking. I realised that this was the first time in my life that I'd had that look from anyone else. I supposed the outfit was working; maybe it made me look older than seventeen. I leaned closer into Nick, and he gave my arm a reassuring rub.

I followed Blake into the house, and we went up and up the stairs until we came out in a loft with big windows and an amazing view.

There were sofas and beanbags spread around one end of the room, vaguely surrounding a big dark coffee table, and lots of music equipment at the other end.

I spotted Scott's blond hair straight away, and panicked, but Nick was right behind me, instantly putting his arm round my waist.

"Jenny! What a surprise, I didn't expect to see you here." Scott came forward to meet us and actually gave me a kiss on the cheek.

The look he gave me wasn't like the one Blake had, but it was warm and friendly. He actually held me away from him and looked at me as though he was seeing me for the first time.

My breath caught, and my stomach did that flip-flop thing.

"I know, right?" Nick broke the moment by pulling me back to his side, away from Scott. "Who would have thought I'd get so lucky?"

I pretended to smile at his words, but my eyes glared at him.

Nick however, seemed oblivious to the daggers coming from my eyes, and dragged me over toward the table to introduce me to everyone else.

There were seven people there, including Scott.

Two other girls and five guys. I recognised Trudy, of course, and gave her a nod, but she looked through me, and focussed her smile on Nick. Damon was there, with a stunning girl I had never seen before, but she gave me a wave and seemed friendly. Damon also looked surprised by the sight of me, but merely gave us a "Hey, Jen, hey, Nick," and jerked his chin up as a greeting.

"Hi, Damon, hi, Rachel," Nick responded. "That's Rachel," he told me, "She's Damon's latest."

"Nick!" Rachel threw a bottle top at him, "Don't say *latest*, it makes me sound like I'll be gone again soon."

Nick grinned at her, "Well, it's true, I expect you'll have dumped him by the end of the night, as soon as you discover how thick he is..." He laughed and ducked as another bottle cap sailed past his head, this time chucked by Damon.

Nick manoeuvred me to a sofa. "That's Dave and that's Tim, they're in the band with Blake." He indicated two men sat opposite, who both said "'Sup," or something equally disinterested, and returned to tuning their guitars.

I was passed a beer, but as I hate beer, I just sipped it for show. I sat next to Nick on the sofa and listened to the conversation flow around me. It was mostly about music. Bands I'd never heard of, let alone seen. Blake, Dave and Tim played some tunes, and without amplifiers it actually sounded okay; at least I could make out some of the lyrics now, which were quite poetic. But in truth I was bored. There was only one reason to stay, but it was a good one.

I kept glancing over at Scott and catching him looking at me. He quickly looked away the first time, but by the third time he grinned instead, knowing full well that I'd noticed.

I quickly dropped my own eyes, but I couldn't help smiling too.

Scott was sitting on a beanbag on the floor with Trudy sat between his legs, leaning back against his chest.

How I envied her!

I tried to be careful about looking at Scott. Trudy could see my face, even though she couldn't see his, and I didn't want to alert her to the fact that he and I were making eye contact.

After about an hour there was some shifting about. Trudy and Rachel went off to the bathroom, and Nick, Damon, Blake and Scott went off to the kitchen to get us all more drinks.

I stretched and after some thought I followed the girls. They were both in the bathroom and I could easily hear them talking through the closed door.

"So what happened to Alice?" That was Rachel's voice.

"I'm not sure. She was supposed to come and see the band on Saturday, but apparently Nick blew her off, and then on Monday he just dumped her without any real explanation." Trudy didn't sound impressed.

"Because of that girl?" Rachel asked.

Trudy snorted. "I doubt it. I mean, she's hardly much to look at compared to Alice, is she? Plus that cutesy act isn't exactly Nick's taste is it? She's probably just a rebound or something."

"Hmmm, I wouldn't be so sure." Rachel sounded thoughtful.

I tiptoed away before they said anything more. I hadn't really needed the bathroom anyway, and I would have died if they'd caught me eavesdropping. But I was shocked by what I'd heard.

Had Nick dumped Alice for me? Surely not. No. No way. He didn't have any feelings for me, and Trudy was right – I wasn't his type. Plus he was only hanging with me to help me get Scott, which was hardly a good reason to dump his girlfriend. Having thought it over, I felt easier in my mind. Nick had dumped Alice for reasons that had nothing to do with me.

I was sitting innocently on the sofa when Nick and Scott and the other girls returned.

"We made you girls some vodka-tonics," Scott said, handing one to Trudy.

Nick put the one he was holding in my hand and took away my barely tasted beer. I was touched by the gesture, as he had obviously suggested it for me; but I didn't really drink normally, and I knew that vodka would probably make me completely spangled.

Once again, Nick surprised me. Sometimes it was like he knew me way better than he actually did.

"Don't worry," he whispered in my ear, "there's no vodka in yours, it's straight tonic water."

I smiled my thanks, more touched than I could say. He patted my knee in a fatherly way, then necked my unwanted beer. I hoped he wasn't planning to get horribly drunk; I was expecting him to walk me home.

After that the evening seemed to go on and on. It was probably still really early, but I was getting ever more bored and tired.

Nick was lounging lengthways on the sofa and I was slumping into him more and more.

The guys from the band began yet another song and I tried to stifle a yawn.

Nick patted the sofa in front of his head.

"Why don't you stretch out, Jones, you look like a poker sat up like that. There's room enough here for both of us."

I looked at the sofa. There wasn't actually a huge amount of room. If I lay down next to Nick then we would be pretty close from head to toe. Though I supposed he was on his back, so it wouldn't really be all that intimate, and I was tired of sitting up.

With a sigh of relief I stretched out. Nick promptly turned on his side, and while his new position did give me a little more room, it also meant that we were now spooning and our bodies were much more intimate than I had intended them to be.

I thought about sitting up again, but I couldn't be bothered to move.

Then I noticed the look on Scott's face. He was staring straight at us and he actually looked kind of annoyed.

I immediately made to move. I didn't want him thinking badly of me.

Nick put one hand firmly on my hip, pressing me deeper into the sofa.

"Don't," he whispered right behind my ear; "that's

exactly how you want him to look. He's finally noticing you, don't blow it now."

I understood what Nick meant. I hadn't thought of it, but having Scott annoyed at Nick cuddling me actually was a good sign. After all, it was the first time he'd shown the slightest bit of jealousy, or any emotion at all really, about me.

I avoided Scott's eyes and tried to relax. My own eyes were beginning to drift closed when I felt Nick's fingertips brushing against my stomach. He was lazily stroking my butterfly tattoo.

"Don't look now, but he's planning how to murder me." Nick's voice was laced with laughter.

Through lowered lids I could see Scott glaring at us. Trudy was trying to get his attention and he was ignoring her. I smiled sleepily and decided not to push his hand away. It felt warm against my bare skin. I wriggled against Nick, trying to get a bit closer to his warmth.

"Uh, Jones?" Nick spoke into my hair.

"Mmm?" I said, half asleep.

"You might want to stop wiggling your bum, or you're going to get a shock."

My eyes shot open. I could suddenly feel exactly what he was talking about, and it was pressing into my rear! I was about to move away, but Nick's fingers were like a clamp around my arm.

"Don't you dare move!" Nick said in a pretend cross voice. "Your body is the only thing covering my dignity. The boys will laugh if you jump up *and* they will see exactly why."

"Then make it go away," I hissed back at him.

"I'm working on it." Nick laughed and soon I felt it recede. I was totally mortified, but secretly a tiny bit flattered. I wasn't sure if I'd ever had that effect on a boy before. When I'd been dating Will he was always trying to get me to put my hand down his pants and "pet his snake", but thankfully I always steered well clear of that particular snake.

I was focussing so much on Nick that I didn't notice that Trudy had finally gotten Scott's attention, and they were now kissing. As soon as I saw it I actually felt sick. Somehow I had managed to convince myself that Scott was noticing me, but now I felt like I'd lost him again. For a short while that evening, Scott had seemed more interested in me and Nick than he was in Trudy. He had definitely been making eye contact with me. But now it was forcefully brought back to me that he was here with her. I wondered if they would be spending the night together somewhere.

"Have you had enough?" Nick asked, sensing my tension.

I nodded and sat up, then stupidly I immediately missed the warmth of this body against mine.

He slung an arm around me, then addressed the group. "I'm going to walk Jenny home. So I'll catch you guys at footie tomorrow?"

There was some banter along the lines of making sure I got home unmolested. The joke being that I wasn't safe from Nick, rather than any muggers on the streets. But I just smiled. I felt completely safe with Nick; he would never try anything without my encouragement. It wasn't as if he liked me that way anyway.

But as we walked in silence along the dark road, I began to rethink. After all, he had shown he was attracted to me; I had felt the attraction up close and personal. I chewed my lip, wondering how to bring it up. I wanted to clear the air because we were friends and I didn't want it to get complicated.

Beside me Nick sighed.

"What?" I asked.

"You're reading too much into it, Jones. You're worrying now, aren't you? You think I'm falling for you, but you only have eyes for Scott?"

"I didn't think that!" It *was* sort of what I was thinking, except that I didn't really think that Nick had feelings for me; I just wasn't his type. But I did want to know what it meant.

Nick ran his hands through his hair as though frustrated. "You're a girl, you're pretty and you were in my arms, it's just biology. No, I don't like you that way."

Good old Nick, he always said just the right thing. I

slipped my arm through his, dissolving the awkward distance between us.

"You know what, Nick? I never realised how nice you were. You have an awful reputation at school as a hard-arse, but you're just a squashy marshmallow underneath, aren't you?"

Nick slapped himself on the forehead. "Only for you, Jones, only for you! God knows why, but you have a way of making people want to do things they wouldn't normally dream of doing. Just don't ever ask me to help you hide a body, because I'm not sure I could say no."

I reached up and kissed him on the cheek. "I won't tell anyone."

"Yeah, make sure of it," he grumbled. "I'd hate to become the go-to guy for every girl who wants some other man."

"It's worth it for Scott, though." I felt the dreamy *I love Scott* look coming over my face.

"Hmm, I think you were getting to him tonight. He couldn't take his eyes off you."

"Do you think so?" I bounced up and down a little. "I thought he was looking over a lot, but then he still seemed pretty intimate with Trudy. What have you said to him to make him interested in me?"

"How do you know I've said anything?" Nick raised an eyebrow.

"Come on, of course you have. He's looking at me now, like properly. It isn't just me turning up with you, you must have said something?"

"Maybe. Just guy stuff though, nothing I can repeat to you." Nick was being evasive.

"Oh go on, please. What did you say?" I wheedled.

"Nope, my lips are sealed. But don't worry your pretty head about it. I'm doing what you asked me to do."

"You're a good friend." I smiled at him.

"Lucky me," he said sarcastically.

I laughed, "Oh dear, this is the second Saturday night in a row you've had to go without getting any action because of me, isn't it?"

"Yup, but as long as you appreciate it then I can

live with it."

"I do," I nodded, "I'll totally make sure you get an A in Science."

"Great." He sounded sarcastic again.

After that, for some weird reason, we spend the rest of the walk home talking about zombies, and where we would go if there was an outbreak. I invited Nick to come and hide at my house because we have a cellar that's impossible to break into, but he said he would rather face a zombie than the torture of being stuck in a cellar with me for weeks on end. Charming!

Outside my house he cupped my face in one hand and I thought he was going to kiss me. But thankfully he didn't; he just stroked my cheek and then said, "See you Monday," and he was gone.

Two Boys, Two Dates

On Monday in the morning I walked into registration unsure if anything would be different. But it was different.

The first thing I noticed, as usual, was Scott. He was sitting with his back to me, but it was almost as though he had been waiting for me to arrive – he turned as soon as I came in and then raised his arm in greeting, giving me the full benefit of his mega-watt Scott smile.

"Hi, Jenny."

I actually wanted to pass out and savour that moment in my dreams forever. Instead I gave him a shy smile and a tentative wave in return.

Damon West turned as well. He was smiling at me too. A really friendly smile. It was all totally surreal. What had I done to make them all like me so much? Just because I'd hung out with them for one Saturday night?

Was I cool now?

I really wished that Nick was in the same registration as us. I needed his banter to relax me. I tried not to trip over any chairs or do anything dumb as I made my way to my usual seat.

Andrea came in a couple of minutes later, but I didn't say anything. I didn't really know what to say anyway. It would sound lame if I said that they had smiled at me and it had felt different.

Andrea and I had spent half of Sunday on the phone. I had told her all about my date, only leaving out the awkward moment between Nick and me on the sofa. I didn't need her going all hyper about that; she was bound to read something into it and say Nick was secretly into me, when I knew he wasn't really.

But I couldn't wait to get to third period science class and tell Nick about the smiling, he'd know exactly what I meant.

When I finally bounced into science I almost hugged Nick, I was that pleased to see him.

"You look happy." He smiled at me.

I nodded. "I am. Scott actually waved at me in

registration this morning, and even Damon was smiling at me like we were friends, and it's all thanks to you."

Nick laughed and blew on his nails, before buffing them on his t-shirt, in a gesture that said, "I know I'm good."

"I've got even better news for you," he said.

"What? Tell me!" I whispered loudly as our teacher glared at me.

I literally had to sit on my hands for the next few minutes as the teacher stamped down the aisle, frowned at us and checked we had our equipment set up, before eventually moving on to annoy someone else.

"Nick!" I poked him hard in the leg with my pencil.

"Okay, okay, you don't need to maim me. Scott broke up with Trudy yesterday."

"You're kidding? That's fantastic. Why, though? What was the reason?"

Nick rolled his eyes at me. "Does it matter? I think he realised she was not the kind of girl he really wanted."

I narrowed my eyes on him suspiciously. "Did he realise that, or did someone else make him realise it? This is your work, isn't it? You totally manipulated him, didn't you?"

"Jones! What a shocking thing to say. If I did, hypothetically of course, then aren't you pleased?"

"I'm completely thrilled. I totally love you!" I bounced up and down on my seat. I absolutely *knew* Nick had been responsible. He was far more conniving than Scott could ever be.

"I take it you mean that you love me in a platonic, what-a-good-friend kind of way?" Nick joked, pretending to be crushed.

"Well, duh, obviously. But I really do; you're amazing, I can't believe you've done all this for me."

"Who says I did this for you? Maybe I did it for Scott? And I'm not admitting to having done anything at all." Nick frowned at his science notes.

I patted his hand. "I know you did. I'm not totally naive."

Nick didn't look at me. "Yes you are, Jennifer Jones, yes you are."

I had no idea what he was talking about, and the teacher was striding over again, so we dropped the subject and focussed on the experiment in front of us.

At afternoon registration Scott walked a long route past my chair to get to his own. He stopped in front of me.

"Hi, Jen. So did you have a good time on Saturday night?"

I looked up into his gorgeous blue eyes and tried not to giggle. "Yes, it was great, thanks."

"Good, good. And Nick got you home okay?"

"Of course." I looked confused. Surely I wouldn't be here if I hadn't gotten home okay?

He looked like he wanted to say more, but he just nodded for a moment and then passed on to his own seat.

Andrea kicked me and waggled her eyebrows. I pulled a "gulp" face and we both laughed. It was a great day.

On Wednesday I had science with Nick again. We worked quietly for a while and then he said, "So, I've been thinking about the final stage of the plan and I think I've got it sussed. Fancy a date with me on Friday?"

I blinked a few times, "A *date* date?"

"No, Jones, not a *date* date, obviously. Scott will be there as well. But you come as my date, and then we have a row, and then you leave. If all goes according to plan then Scott should go after you."

"Really? You think you can orchestrate that to happen?" I was amazed he was so confident of pulling something like that off.

"Yes, but listen, you can't invite Andrea. If she comes along and then you leave, she is bound to be the one who goes after you, okay?"

"Uh, sure." I didn't think it would be a problem anyway. Andrea and Brad seemed to be getting pretty heavy. Andrea claimed it wasn't the romance of the century or anything like that, but I had a feeling she was really falling for him and too embarrassed to tell me yet.

As Nick began to fill me in on the details of his plan, I was both really nervous and excited. I wasn't at all sure it would work, but Nick just smiled at my doubts.

So on Friday night I got ready for my "date" with Nick. It was a hot summer evening and a group of kids were meeting by the river. There was a wide grassy bank that was always full of people having picnics during the weekend, but on Friday night it was a "cool kids" hangout.

I'd even heard stories about people skinny-dipping in the river late at night, presumably after a few drinks or for a dare. I knew there was no chance of me doing that, but I deliberately wore dark colours, despite the heat, so I wouldn't get any obvious grass stains or anything on my clothes.

The river wasn't far from my house, so I said I'd meet Nick there, and it was still practically broad daylight when I got there at around eight-thirty. I recognised our lot straight away. Four picnic rugs had been grouped together and everyone was lying around on them, drinking and chatting.

There *were* people swimming in the river, but no one I recognised, and thankfully they all appeared to be wearing clothes!

I gave Nick a wave when I saw him, and then another towards Scott, as I saw him sitting near Nick. It was so nice to see him relaxing without Trudy draped all over him.

Nick knocked the top off a bottle of cider and handed it to me, and I sank down next to him and sipped gratefully, as it was still ice cold.

I let the chat flow around me for a while. Nick and Damon were arguing about who was going in goal for their football team on Sunday, and Scott appeared to be listening, but then he suddenly started talking to me. He sidled closer and asked how I was doing, and had I done the homework yet from English class.

It was weird, but I was thrilled. I answered as best I could, trying to remember what I'd written about *Great Expectations* for English, but in my head I was really trying to work out if he was interested in me. Was he just talking to me because he was friendly? Was he talking to me because I was there with Nick? Was he talking to me because I had somehow become part of their cool group?

He started to ask more personal questions, like what did I read for pleasure, and what was my favourite class, and if I did any sports. I couldn't really remember any boy taking that much interest in me, ever.

Nick suddenly stopped talking and turned his attention on us. His stare was cold enough that Scott lifted his head off his hands.

"What?" he asked Nick.

"Would you mind very much not hitting on my date?" Nick said with a nasty edge to his voice.

Scott looked surprised, but I wasn't; I'd been expecting something like this, it was part of the plan. My stomach began to twist into sick knots at what was coming.

Scott put up his hands, "Mate, I'm not hitting on

her, we were just chatting."

Nick glared at him, "Don't you think it's bad enough that she'd rather be here with you than me? You both think I don't know the way you look at each other?"

I made a moan of embarrassment and covered my red face with my hands. This wasn't exactly how I'd thought this would go. I didn't think my feelings were going to get outed!

Nick pulled my hands down. "It's true, isn't it Jenny? Scott's the reason that I can never get anywhere with you?"

"No," I whispered, feeling completely mortified.

"Oh, right," he said, still in that bitter tone. "So you're here for me? Come on then, Jen, show me a bit of affection." He pulled me close, one arm sliding down my back and the other round my neck, pulling me in for a kiss. I pushed away from him.

"Stop it, Nick! We're just friends, okay? I keep telling you that." This was a line I was supposed to say.

"Yeah, well, that's fine. But don't expect me to play

the third wheel any more, either of you. I have bigger fish to fry! And good luck to the both of you, you deserve each other." Nick said it like he was mad, but really I knew he was trying to indicate that he gave his blessing.

I jumped up, pretending to be really upset, and said tearfully, "I'm going home. Don't bother walking me, Nick, I can manage on my own."

As I walked away I heard Scott calling Nick a bunch of names that he didn't deserve.

I was about halfway home before I heard Scott calling after me. I couldn't believe it; the plan had worked! I stopped to let him catch up.

"I just wanted to make sure you got home okay," he said.

"Thanks." I smiled at him and we continued walking. The silence seemed to stretch out for a several minutes before Scott cleared his throat awkwardly.

"So you and Nick, I thought you guys were getting together?"

I shook my head, "No, we're just friends; I don't like him that way."

Scott looked at me sideways, "Are you sure? I mean a lot of girls like Nick, *that way*; he has the bad boy thing down pat."

I laughed, "Yeah, he won't be lonely for long. He is hot, but not my type."

"So was he right? Do you maybe like someone else?" Scott asked.

"Maybe," I kept my eyes on my feet as I walked, too embarrassed to look at him.

"Or maybe you aren't actually into boys at all? I know a couple of girls you might quite like instead."

I stopped still in surprise, and goggled at him. It was only then that I saw his big blue eyes were full of teasing laugher.

I gave him a punch on the arm. "Yes, I like boys, and yes, I like someone in particular." I said bravely.

"So if I asked you out, might I get a yes?" Scott said, still teasing.

I think I blushed right to the tips of my ears. "Yes,"

I said.

"Tomorrow night?" Scott continued. "A proper date. Dinner at La Reine perhaps?"

I nodded, too overcome with joy to speak. We grinned at each other for a long moment.

After that we didn't talk much. It was only another couple of minutes to my house, and all too soon we were standing outside.

"So I'll see you tomorrow?" Scott said, "Do you want to meet there? I'm in town in the afternoon anyway, but I can swing back and get you in a taxi if you want?"

"No, don't be daft. I'll meet you there." I knew I could get my dad to drive me; he was pretty good about that sort of thing. "What time?"

"Around eight?" Scott suggested, and I nodded.

"Cool." Scott took my hands and I waited for him to kiss me. But he didn't. He kissed my hand instead. I actually shivered, it was so romantic.

"I'll see you tomorrow. Sleep well." He dropped my hands.

"Thanks for walking me home. Goodnight." I walked up to the front door, fishing out my key, as quickly as I could. I wanted to spin the moment out, but at the same time I didn't want it to turn awkward again. So I figured it was better to make a quick exit and leave it perfect.

I gave him one more wave as I opened the door, then shut it behind me and sagged against it in utter elation.

Scott Lawes had asked me out! On a real date! I was so happy I felt like I could fly up the stairs.

The Kiss

I put in earbuds and silently danced to tunes from my favourite musical as I changed into my pyjamas. It wasn't even ten o'clock, but I just wanted to go to bed and relive every moment of the walk home in my mind, over and over.

I brushed my teeth and then switched off the music, and climbed into bed. I started flicking through books on my Kindle, trying to find something that might hold my attention, but I couldn't find a singe thing that was good enough to distract me from thinking about Scott. In the end I just lay there and stared at the ceiling with a massive grin on my face.

My parents go to bed really early because my dad usually has to be up at about five for his commute to London, so I was instantly alert when I heard a strange noise at around eleven that night.

I leaped a mile as a stone dinged off my window. I rushed over and pushed the window open.

In the shadows of the front garden I could make

out a figure.

"Who's that?" I whispered cautiously.

"It's me, Nick." He answered.

"Hang on, I'll be right down." I didn't stop for a dressing gown or slippers, because the night was so warm, but I did briefly pull a brush through my hair; after all, Nick was still a boy! I glanced down at my so-called pyjamas. I was wearing a faded Lord of the Rings t-shirt that went almost to my knees (extra large was the only size they had left at the cinema when I eventually got into the premier) and a pair of boxer shorts underneath. I figured it was all fairly good coverage, if perhaps a little bit lame, but it was only Nick so I didn't bother to change.

I slipped out the front door, leaving it on the latch behind me, and walked barefoot through the grass to where Nick was waiting on the swing under our apple trees.

I threw my arms around him. "You did it! Thank you so much! Did Scott come back to the river afterwards? He asked me out!" I squealed in his ear as

I hugged him.

Nick chuckled at my enthusiasm and let me hug him.

"Are you wearing a bra?" he asked after a minute. I jumped away and was suddenly aware of the fact I'd been pressing myself against him.

"Uh, no," I said self-consciously.

"Thought not." Nick gave me one of his lascivious looks. But I was so happy that I didn't even smack him like I normally would.

"Don't wind me up," I said fondly. "Right now I freaking adore you. You are without doubt the smartest male in the whole world. And you got me Scott! You didn't just make him notice me, he's asked me out! To dinner at La Reine tomorrow night. What can I do to thank you? If there is anything at all I can do for you in return, just name it."

"La Reine?" Nick's eyebrows went up. "I can't remember the last time he liked a girl enough to take her for an actual meal."

"Well, it's just pizza and stuff, you know," I said

coyly.

"Hmmm, so did he kiss you?" Nick asked.

I blushed in the darkness. "No, but he kissed my hand." I sighed again at how romantic it was.

"Oh, bleh!" Nick scoffed, "That's a bit cheesy, isn't it?"

"No," I said moodily.

Nick pulled me a little closer. He was sat on the swing and I was stood almost between his legs.

"I'm glad he didn't kiss you properly," he said in a low voice, "I wanted to be first."

"Huh?" I looked at him in confusion.

"I want you to kiss me," Nick clarified.

"What? Why?" I tried to step back but he didn't let go.

Nick shrugged. "Because you said you would do something for me in return. Because I've not kissed a girl in two weeks, dancing attendance on you. Because it's late and I've been drinking and I want you to. It's how I want you to thank me."

"Don't you think it's a bad idea? I mean, what

would Scott think if I say yes to going out with him and then made out with you? Talk about sending mixed messages! I can't play games and not care like you can."

I said all that, but a small part of me suddenly really wanted to kiss Nick. I wasn't sure where it came from. Maybe the sexy way he was looking at me, or how full his lips were, or how deep his dark eyes were; but suddenly I really wanted him to make me do it.

"You said you would do anything I wanted in return for my help. *Just name it,*" he mimicked me. "All I want is for you to kiss me, just once, like you mean it. I'm not going to tell Scott. He'll never know."

"But why?" I persisted.

"Shut up and kiss me, Jones." Nick gave my t-shirt a hard tug, pulling me towards him, while his other hand cupped my behind, forcing me even closer between his legs and against his rock-hard chest. We were at eye level and he paused for just a second, making eye contact with me. There was no humour in his gaze at all. Just a raw need.

I felt him take a deep breath and then he swooped straight in on my lips.

I kept my mouth shut for only a second and then I gave into my own secret desire and kissed him back.

I kissed him like I meant it, not just because he asked me to, but because I couldn't help it.

His kiss was bone-melting.

My knees went to jelly and my brain went to mush. My arms twined themselves around his neck and my lips demanded more. It was like I couldn't get close enough. He tasted of beer and mints. His tongue danced with mine, and I sucked at his bottom lip like it was cookie dough. My whole body began to sag into his until he lifted me with both hands and settled me on his lap, never taking his lips off mine, my legs either side of his on the swing.

One of his hands snaked inside my t-shirt and found the bare skin of my breasts. I groaned but didn't stop. Instead I wrapped my legs firmly around his waist, trying to get even closer.

"Whoa, Jen." It was Nick who pulled away. He

blew out a breath. I was that shameless that I merely looked at him blankly for a moment before going in for another kiss. He leaned back and avoided my lips.

He lifted me off his lap, scooting out from under me and leaving me sat on the swing alone. He ran his hands through his dark hair several times and swore softly under his breath.

My own brain felt like it was covered in treacle. I couldn't think at all. I just stared at him, willing him to kiss me again, but somehow knowing I wasn't supposed to. I couldn't quite remember why.

I shook my head; it seemed dazed by lust.

"Sorry," I said eventually, when it became obvious that I had somehow put him off and he wasn't going to kiss me again.

"No, I'm sorry, Jen. That was totally out of order of me. It's one thing to kiss you, but I think even Scott would be pretty unforgiving if I shagged his new girlfriend the night before your first date."

I bit my lip. "I wasn't going to do that!"

"Hah, could have fooled me, Jones; seems like you

wanted it to me."

I looked at the floor. I did want it, or some of it, whatever it was. I didn't really have any experience, but I knew I wanted more. But the mention of Scott cleared my brain a little.

What was I doing? I loved Scott – why was I passionately kissing Nick?

I didn't even fancy Nick, did I?

Hmmm – my body said yes, clearly I did. My brain said no, I only wanted Scott.

"I'd better go." Nick moved closer and put one hand on my shoulder.

Treacherous tart that I was, I lifted my face up, just in case he might like to kiss me again.

He didn't.

Instead he gave my shoulder a squeeze. "Have a good time tomorrow. We'll talk more next week, okay?"

I nodded, feeling suddenly dejected as he slipped out of my garden and walked away into the darkness.

I crept back upstairs to bed, trying to recapture

Stella Wilkinson

some of the high I had felt when Scott had gone.

After a while I began to smile. Just the thought of Scott, gorgeous, funny Scott, made me happy inside and out. I hugged myself. Tomorrow night I was going on my first date with Scott. I lay awake for ages thinking about him and how wonderful life was going to be from now on.

When I eventually fell asleep I dreamed of Nick...

Part 2 – Nick

Stella Wilkinson

Jonesing

I like having Jennifer Jones for my lab partner, mainly because she does all the work. It's not that I'm bad at science, far from it in fact; but Jenny is so enthusiastic, and I just like watching her. She has one of those totally expressive faces, you can see exactly what she's thinking all the time. It's like she hasn't learned yet how to hide her feelings. Most girls are good at faking expressions, pretending to be interested in sport, or pretending to be coy when you know they are up for it, or the one I really hate – fake pouting when they don't get their own way. Jenny doesn't do any of those. She is just simply Jenny.

The only class we have together is Science, but I've sat next to her twice a week for two years now. I've learned that she gets excited when she gets the answers, that she likes explaining it to me, and that she's totally cute when she concentrates.

She's isn't girlfriend material, though. She'd get hurt

too easily. Maybe one day, when she's a bit more grown-up and not such an innocent. Though actually I would hate her to change. I like her being exactly the way she is.

So it came as a surprise in class when I could see she was really struggling to concentrate on the experiment we were doing. Instead she seemed edgy, like she wanted to ask me something but didn't have the nerve.

I watched her dither for a few minutes just for the fun of it, then prompted her.

"Spit it out, Jones."

You could have knocked me down with a feather when she wanted to know what I was doing at the weekend. She had never shown any interest in my personal life, though actually I don't think I'd ever shown much interest in hers either.

I gave her one of my "checking-her-out" looks, because she always blushes when I do, which is cute beyond words; but I chose my next words carefully. I was curious as to why she was interested. Was she interested in me? Was she just making conversation? Was she just bored and lonely this weekend or was the question leading up to something else? I had a think and came up with three different ways to test which way this was going.

"Stop it." She flicked her pen at me.

"What?" I said innocently, but laughing inside.

"Stop acting like I said something crude!" She was still blushing.

"Jones. You insult me. I'm merely curious about this sudden interest in my plans, and whether you might finally have started appreciating the perfection that sits beside you." I tried for a teasing tone, but actually I wondered if she did have a bit of a crush on me, in which case I would have to tread carefully. I didn't want to hurt her feelings but I was currently dating Alice, and Alice was holding my interest rather nicely at present. She was ballsy and adventurous, but she was lacking that soft femininity that Jenny had in spades.

"Oh, get over yourself. You know I have zero

interest in your massive over-inflated ego! Just forget it." Jenny turned back to our experiment as if she were sulking.

"Sorry, go on, what is you really want to know? That I was thinking of watching the 'Supernatural' marathon on TV this weekend?" This one was to test if she wanted to spend the time snuggling up with me; watching 'Supernatural' would be an acceptable excuse to any girl. "Or that I'm hanging with friends at The Coach House Saturday night?" I mentioned this because she might be wanting to expand her social life and maybe find another boyfriend; after all, it had been a couple of months since her breakup with Will Dobright. "Or that I'm playing five-a-side on Sunday morning? Which bit of that might be worthy of discussion to you?" I threw in the last one in case she had a thing for Damon – so many girls do – and they think that coming to watch the football will somehow get him to like them more.

She paused for only a second. "The Coach House?" she said.

Interesting, I thought. "You want to come?"

"Are you inviting me?" she asked, which was so sweet; it's not as though she needed an invitation, but I'd never seen her there before. Maybe she needed to be reassured there would be friendly faces there, or maybe she actually did want to spend more time with me?

"Like a date?" I said, double-checking.

"No. Not like a date! I just… thought I should get out there a bit more, you know? Mingle."

Oh, *mingle*. I knew what mingle meant, it meant there *was* someone she wanted to see more of, but it wasn't me.

"Who is he?"

"I don't know what you're talking about," she hedged.

"Come on, Jones. You can tell me. You're obviously not hankering for *my* bod or you would have gone with the 'Supernatural' marathon. Who do you really want to see more of?"

"I might have a tiny crush on Scott," she whispered,

like it was a dirty secret.

I couldn't help laughing. She obviously had a massive crush, not a tiny one, or she wouldn't have risked saying anything to me. After all, Scott was one of my best mates, and usually I would have no hesitation in telling him about it straight away, but she was just too vulnerable. She was the kind of girl who would rather disappear into the floor than be obvious about her crush. I don't know why but I wanted to spare her the embarrassment. On the other hand, Scott was single right now, and he might actually be interested. After all, Jenny wasn't unattractive; quite pretty really, just a bit of a shy wallflower.

"Have you tried just telling him? Scott isn't that scary. He doesn't have girls queuing round the block, well, not masses; he might be flattered."

"No," she said, "I just can't. It would be too embarrassing. Right now I just want him to notice me. And if you want to pass Chemistry, you have to promise to keep your mouth shut, okay?"

"Whatever you say, Jones, and of course you're

invited on Saturday night. Bring Andrea. The band will probably be lame, but we'll have fun anyway."

She seemed happy with that. But as we went back to our experiment I pondered the problem of her shyness and its consequent invisibility cloak. Scott was a good guy, but recently I had noticed a distinct leaning in him towards the kind of girls I usually dated. He wasn't exactly a trendsetter, and over the years I had often noticed he followed where I led. Last year it had been my shoes and the style of my jeans. His copying was one of the reasons I had switched to black clothes; they looked too harsh with his blond hair and he knew it. The girls thing might have been a coincidence, but I didn't think so. Jenny was actually perfect for him, but he had been pursuing relationships recently with more aggressive, confident girls – my type of girls in fact. I even suspected he had an eye on Trudy, an ex with whom I'd recently had a brief but torrid fling thing. If he was going to keep copying my taste in girls then Jenny didn't stand a chance; she was from a totally different mould. I wondered if there was anything I could do to help her. I could subtly suggest to Scott that she was a goer, but I didn't think Jenny would appreciate that somehow. Maybe the key was to get her to break her mould a little.

"He doesn't see you as a girl, you know."

"What?" She looked surprised, and I felt mean, but I was only trying to help her.

"You're too sweet. Like someone's little sister. You need to start by making him aware that you're all grown up now."

She bit her lip, emphasising how adorable she was.

"How?" she asked.

I gave her another once-over. "Do you own any outfits that are a bit less conservative? It will be a night out, can you sex it up a bit?"

"Scott isn't like that," she said defensively.

I couldn't help but laugh; we were talking about a seventeen-year-old boy, did she really think he wasn't going to be checking out her rack? "We're all like that, honey-pie, it's how we're built."

I watched the thoughts play across her face, from feeling unsure to bullying herself into a decision.

"Yeah, I can do that." she confirmed.

Poor kid. I suddenly felt I would do anything to help her. She was putting herself right out of her comfort zone to impress Scott. I just hoped he appreciated what he could have.

Over the next couple of days I found myself thinking about Jenny and Scott, and wondering if The Coach House was really such a good idea. She was probably just setting herself up for a major rejection. She wasn't even on his radar right now. He didn't know her like I did, he didn't know what a perfect girlfriend she would be for someone like him. Scott needed his ego stroked a lot, and Jenny would be suitably faithful and adoring.

I was also wondering if it was such a good idea to have invited her, because Alice would throw a fit if she found out. Alice was pretty possessive and not scared of letting other girls know if they were overstepping the line, in her opinion. The more I thought about it, the worse the idea seemed. If Alice found out that it was me that invited Jenny, then she would take it out on Jenny. Maybe even threaten her to stay away, and I didn't want to expose Jenny to that.

Which meant I either had to tell Jenny that I had changed my mind or tell Alice that I wasn't seeing her on Saturday night after all. Neither option seemed appealing. But in the end my pathetically soft heart won out. Alice would get over it, Jenny might not. So I tracked down Alice and told her that I was just hanging with the guys on Saturday and would she mind if we hooked up another night, but she went mental at me. It was kind of off-putting. I knew she didn't really want to see the any of the bands that were playing because she'd already declared them all "crap", but she was totally not cool about it. We left things kind of frosty, and I even wondered if she would turn up anyway, but there wasn't much more I could do about it.

I kept asking myself why on earth I was bothering to go through all this for Jenny Jones, but one look at her excited and hopeful face on Saturday night and I knew exactly why.

To Flirt Or Not To Flirt...

I was kind of hoping that Jenny wouldn't come to The Coach House after all. I was fifty-fifty on whether she would bail, so I hadn't mentioned her coming to my mates. Then Scott hooked up with Trudy at the bar, and by the time they got back to our table, they were all over each other.

Trudy was what my older brother Mike would call "suitably damaged". She had issues with guys and didn't trust them, but that didn't stop her from wanting to lay as many of them as she could. I met her through a friend in a band when she was sleeping with him. I remember him saying "She leaves you tired and happy, but unsure if you managed to please her in return. " I like that kind of challenge, and when she set her sights on me, I was determined to make sure I pleased her. Ha! I didn't stand a chance; she made me constantly feel as if I was doing something wrong. She was as vocal out of bed as in it, always shouting at me for something. In the end I decided that she wasn't worth it, but we ended amicably, and I should have known she would be here tonight.

To be honest, I didn't think that Scott would interest her – he was too sporty and clean cut – but then he did have a good physique; maybe she thought he'd have a lot of stamina.

She was practically straddling him at the table and he was looking half scared, half thrilled, when I saw Jenny arrive.

I actually felt guilty, like I should have kept Scott in check for her, but really, there was nothing I could have done. Trudy was like a shark when she knew what she wanted; the only thing I could do now was to soften the blow a little.

When I saw Jenny's face I actually wished she was there for me and not for Scott. That look of anticipation in her smile, the slight nervousness in the way she bit her lip, the hopeful light in her eyes. No one had ever felt all that about seeing me. Plus she looked smokin'. She had taken my words to heart and was wearing a pale blue summer dress, displaying long legs at the bottom and a low square neckline at the top; she was finally showing some flesh and could easily pass for over eighteen. Her makeup was still minimal, but she had such creamy skin that she didn't really need it. Maybe she could use a bit more around the eyes to emphasise them, they were such a nice green-grey colour.

I gave Jenny a welcoming smile and she seemed quite glad to see me, even though I could see that she was gutted about Scott. I made her sit down between me and Damon to show everyone that she was part of the group, and I made some flirty comments to make her laugh. It didn't take her long to revert to her usual good humour.

My biggest problem now was actually trying to restrain myself from flirting with her for real. That would be a complication that neither of us needed. She was totally smitten with Scott, and also I didn't want to jeopardise my friendship with her by coming across like a horn-dog. So I tried to keep the flirting light, just enough to make her feel good but not too much. But man, it was hard. She was sitting really close to me and she smelled amazing, like a fresh honeydew melon.

I needed another drink. I signalled for a waitress.

"A beer for me, please. What will you have, Jones? A lager top? Or maybe a cider?"

Jenny pinched me under the table. I knew she didn't really drink, but I figured she could use one to loosen up, so I ordered her a half of cider anyway.

Within minutes Jenny's good mood was starting to wane again. It didn't help that Scott seemed oblivious to her presence, he was so overwhelmed by Trudy's rather more blatant sexuality. I tried not to get annoyed by how often her eyes travelled over to them instead of focussing on me.

Scott was petting Trudy's dragon tattoo and I could see Jenny trying to work out why he liked it.

"Yes, Jones, it is sexy."

"What?"

"The tattoo. It's sexy. It isn't the kind of thing you want a girl to display in front of your mother, and maybe it is a tiny bit trampy, but do you really think a seventeen-year-old boy cares? Perhaps you should get one." I didn't really mean it, certainly not a real one, but I would bet good money it would pull Scott's attention briefly away from Trudy. It would just be so unexpected and kind of "nice girl but naughty" on Jenny.

I noticed Jenny was suddenly staring over my shoulder and turned to see what she was looking at. Her friend Andrea was tickling Brad's tonsils with her tongue, and the look on Jenny's face was priceless.

"Everyone but you, huh?" I teased.

"I was just surprised; she said she didn't like Brad. And anyway, *you're* not with anyone tonight!"

I scooted even closer, "Actually, Jones, I'm pretty sure that most of the people around us think I'm just about to score."

We had been talking only to each other for half an hour now, and I had pretty much ignored my mates, focussing all my attention on her. Yeah, I was confident that they all thought I was on the pull, and that any minute now I'd be in there.

Obviously none of this had occurred to Jenny, because the moment I pointed it out, her eyes went straight to Scott as if she had been doing something wrong, and she shifted away from me.

I rolled my eyes and dragged her close again. "Jeez, Jenny. You really don't know much about boys, do you! Boys want what other boys have. If someone else wants something then you begin to think about that thing. You realize you should be the one to have it. We are childish like that. If no one wants the thing, then it would never occur to us that it might be desirable."

I tried to explain to her that Scott would be more interested in her if he thought that I was after her. I couldn't really tell her that he tends to copy me, as that would have made me a bad mate, but I could try to make her see that my attention would only increase her attractiveness to other boys.

I wasn't even sure why I was trying to convince her. It would all require even more effort on my part, and I failed to see what was in it for me. But for some reason I wanted to help Jenny, maybe even spend more time with her. I was growing to like the girl more with every minute we spent together.

She was quiet for a minute, thinking over what I'd said. I wondered if she would work out that I was offering to play the fake suitor, or if I'd been too subtle.

"Do you have a girlfriend?" she suddenly asked, catching me off guard. "Are you still seeing Alice?"

I almost choked on my beer. Damn, I hadn't even thought about Alice. I'd already royally ticked her off by cancelling our date tonight, and now I was merrily flirting with Jenny as though she was going to be Alice's replacement. Alice would turn on Jenny if I didn't cut company with one of them. I had to make a choice and quickly!

My current girlfriend, who I had been getting on just fine with, and who let me do all kinds of lusty things to her – or this shy girl who wanted nothing at all from me except friendship?

"No. And don't ask nosy questions."

Did I really just say that? Did I really just tell Jenny

that I wasn't going out with Alice anymore? Why on earth had I made that call? I tell you, this girl could sell sand to Arabia just by batting her eyelashes.

"Nick?" she said at last, "You know what you were saying about Scott wanting me more if other boys liked me as well?"

I groaned and slapped my forehead. "*Is* that what I was saying?" I said, even though that was exactly what I had meant.

"So, would you do that for me?" she asked.

"What *exactly* do you want me to do?" I hooked a finger down the front of her top and got a good eyeful of her small but perfect cleavage. "Shall I show everyone that I think that you're hot by groping you in public maybe? Or perhaps we could just kiss for a while, or you could come sit on my lap?" I teased.

"It's okay, you don't actually have to do any of those things. Just maybe drop it into conversation that you think I'm cute or something?"

Oh, if only she knew. She was most definitely cute and I'd only been half kidding.

"So I don't get any kisses? Not even fake passion? Surely I should at least get to feel your boobs? Otherwise what's in it for me?"

"You get all my gratitude," she said sweetly, "which should be reflected in your science grade."

Oh joy, I thought sarcastically. That will keep me warm at night. But I merely agreed and told her she would need to at least act a little bit interested in me, despite the fact that I knew she only had eyes for Scott.

I didn't know how to say it nicely, but basically she had to act a little bit like she actually liked boys. We all knew that Will Dobright had left her because he wasn't getting anywhere with her, and I didn't think that kind of reputation was particularly helpful, no matter how secretly glad I was that she hadn't given anything up to that creep.

So we continued to talk, and I continued to try not to flirt with her even though I had this overwhelming temptation to make her blush again. But I kept myself in check – after all, what would be the point? She really wasn't interested in anyone but Scott.

She was nearly finished with her half and I was about to order her another drink, when I realised she was scanning the dance floor for Scott.

I sighed and asked, "Would you like to dance?"

She almost leaped up, she was so keen to find him.

We had a few awkward moments on the dance floor. I desperately wanted to press my body against hers and really move to the music, but she would have freaked, so left a respectable distance between us, and touched her as little as possible.

We moved closer and closer to Scott. He was getting pretty friendly with Trudy and my instinct was to leave them to it, but I supposed it wouldn't hurt to let him see me dancing with Jenny.

When he did finally notice who I was with he raised his eyebrows at me in surprise. I gave him a "Look what I got!" smug grin.

His eyes said, "Nice one. Have you scored?"

"Not for the want of trying," I answered out loud.

Scott winked at Jenny and said, "Keep up the good

work."

I was pleased with the exchange. I'd set the scene, showing my interest in her. I would still have to sell her a little to the boys, but soon they would all wonder what she had that had captured my attention.

I started to walk Jenny back to our table, but she'd had enough and wanted to go home. I joked about how I would have to be on my best behaviour for the rest of the night, but she didn't really get it. Little did she know how true it was. Plus I was now actually going to have to dump my girlfriend in the morning!

Jenny hugged me. "Thanks again for inviting us tonight. I don't think it was a total bust, " she said.

"No, I don't think it was." I said. Not for her anyway…

Setting The Scene

On Sunday morning I had a five-a-side footie with Damon, Paul, Mike and Spudhead (I've never even asked what his real name is). After the game we all walked to the café on the green, where we could sit outside in the sun and re-hydrate. Mike went home, but it wasn't long before Scott finished his swim practice and joined us instead.

The five of us shunned the chairs and instead stretched out on the grass. There was some talk about football and then as usual it switched to girls.

First we ribbed Scott about Trudy, that if he was really lucky then she'd eat him for breakfast and not spit him out. There was much laughter over that.

Damon took some flak about rejecting several girls the night before. He was hot for a girl called Rachel who had only just broken up with her previous boyfriend and wanted some "time", which meant that Damon had to cool his heels if he wanted to show her he was serious. We all liked Rachel; she didn't go to our school but she was Scott's next-door neighbour and so we'd known her forever. She was a stunner, and if I'd been Scott I would have been working the connection on a daily basis. But apparently they had tried dating when they were eleven and it had been too weird, like brother and sister, or some such nonsense. But I suppose that was good news for Damon.

Then they rounded on me.

"So, did you and Alice have a fight?" Scott said.

"Yeah, and what was with you hanging all over that other chick? Jennifer something?" Damon added.

"Jones," I said, avoiding the Alice question; "her name is Jennifer Jones. She's my science lab partner."

Spudhead looked surprised, "The girl from last night? She was a science nerd? She looked hot to me."

"She's not a science nerd, just my partner in Science class. And yes, she is kind of hot, isn't she?" I knew I had to go carefully here. If I overdid the enthusiasm then the other boys, including Scott, would totally back off and give me a clear field, so I had to sound keen but not *too* keen. I basically just wanted to plant the seed in Scott's mind that Jenny was a contender.

"She's got a certain something, I dunno what, but it's sexy…" I let them all think about it for a second before continuing. "But she's not really my usual type; we'll see."

"But she's single, right?" Spudhead downed his soda. "That makes her my type."

"Just having a pulse makes her your type," I teased.

"So you didn't get anywhere?" Scott asked me.

"No, she's not like Trudy. Jenny isn't a one-night stand kind of girl. She's real girlfriend material, you know? A keeper if you can get her."

Damon smirked at me. "She's got no chance against you. You'll get her if you want her."

I pretended to mull that over. "I'm not so sure," I said slowly. "I have the feeling she already likes someone else." I let my eyes rest on Scott for a moment, until I was sure he noticed.

Time for a subject change. I had done what Jenny had asked. I had built her up in the eyes of the boys, and I had even hinted to Scott that he might do better with her than I could, and I'd managed to malign Trudy all in the same breath. It was maybe a bit mean, seeing as I knew Scott was swayed by the opinions of Damon and me, but it would make Jenny happy.

On Monday morning Scott and I had French together.

He was all hyper because Trudy had come over to his house the night before and rocked his mattress for him. I had to listen to an almost blow-by-blow account of what she could do in bed. I tried to refrain from pointing out that I'd already dated her and was more than familiar with her skill set, but it was bad news for Jenny, because this was one area that she had no chance of competing in against Trudy. So instead I was openly crude about Trudy's prowess, saying I'd seen it all and more, and basically making her sound like she would turn tricks for dog biscuits. Trudy didn't really deserve it, but I couldn't see her relationship with Scott lasting long anyway. She needed someone stronger to hold her interest.

I'm not sure how much of it penetrated through Scott's post-coital happy haze, but I'd done what I could to put him off. At the end of the day, it was going to be his choice. I didn't mind giving him a bit of a nudge, but I wasn't going to completely manipulate my friend. Even though Jenny was clearly the better choice for him.

Scott continued to talk about Trudy for most of the rest of the lesson. "So, Trudy is friends with Blake from that band we saw on Saturday, and he's invited us to his place this Saturday, and he has a spare room that Trudy says she and I could crash in."

"Yeah, I know Blake," I nodded. "And the other guys from the band. It'll be pretty dull, they just sit around and play music and expect us to tell them how great it sounds."

"Say you'll come, dude. I want to spend a whole night with Trudy." Scott gave me a pleading look.

"Yeah, sure. Maybe I'll invite Jones," I said, casually.

"So it's over with you and Alice then?" Scott said.

Damn. I'd forgotten about Alice. "Yeah, it's over." I didn't elaborate. I'd have to track her down asap and break the news, before she heard it from someone else. I couldn't invite Jenny on Saturday and keep dating Alice as well. Alice would have my balls if I did.

The question I should have been pondering was why I decided I'd invite Jenny and not Alice? But I didn't want to look too closely at my motives. Instead I just shrugged to myself. Jenny had a way of making me want to help her. Yes, as I said to the boys, she definitely had a certain something...

Not So Fake Feelings After All

When I picked Jenny up at the end of her road on Saturday night, I almost had a coronary. She looking freaking fantastic. Her jeans were low-slung and her top was cut off just under her boobs, showing a delicious expanse of smooth, toned stomach that I just wanted to lick. She'd even put a little butterfly on her belly, which I couldn't resist petting. Her sweet expression and her sinful body were like a siren call to men. How could anyone resist such a mixture? Scott surely wouldn't be able to resist her after seeing her like this. I wasn't sure if I could either!

Down, boy! I growled silently to myself. I thought she'd looked hot last Saturday in the summer dress, but now that she'd ditched adorable and gone with sexy, it was a whole other level of temptation. But this stunning transformation wasn't for my benefit, and I would do well to remember that.

I wondered if she had even overdone it a bit when we got to Blake's house and he started giving her the eye. He was looking at her like she was a tasty treat, and it annoyed the hell out of me.

I glared at him, which I was allowed to do, because Jenny was officially my date, but he just smirked at me before watching her arse sway up the stairs. I couldn't help watching it myself.

I mentally slapped my own cheek. Why was I suddenly feeling possessive of Jenny? The whole point of the night was to help her get the attention of another guy. I couldn't suddenly want her for myself just because she looked good tonight, could I? Was I really that shallow? Jenny and I were friends. I liked her as a person. Could I have a friend that I now found attractive? Yes. After all, I thought lots of girls were attractive, and I didn't have to date them all.

But the closer I got to Jenny, the more I liked her. Why did I have to wait until we were in this dumb situation before I realised that?

It really didn't help that Scott looked so pleased to see her – when we entered Blake's loft, Scott got straight to his feet and came over to meet us.

I say us, but in fact he only had eyes for Jenny. Some of my comments from earlier in the week must have sunk in a little, because he definitely seemed to be looking at her in a whole new light. As though she was some mystery he wanted to solve. I could actually see it happening, and I didn't like it. But this is what was supposed to happen.

I couldn't help myself. I reclaimed Jenny from Scott as soon as decently possible; wrapping my arm around her waist, I dragged her away on the pretext of introducing her to everyone else.

I could feel Jenny glaring at me. I had just spoiled a *moment* between her and Scott, but I pretended not to notice.

It was a relief when we all chilled out to listen to some music, so I could try and get my thoughts in order.

My mind was like a pendulum. Jenny and Scott were at one end, then the pendulum would swing the other way, to Jenny and me. Was that possible? Jenny didn't like me that way. I didn't like her that way, or did I now? How seriously? Enough to risk getting involved long-term? It couldn't be any other way, not with Jenny.

No, I didn't like her enough to want to shackle myself to just one girl for the foreseeable future. Much better to stick to the plan. Jenny and Scott. They were perfect for each other. Jenny was so nice and normal, Scott was so nice and normal. She would be supportive of his sports, always there for him, but not too needy. That sounded so good, I'd like that in a girlfriend for myself.

But at the end of the day, it didn't matter what I wanted; it mattered what Jenny wanted. She didn't want me, she wanted Scott.

Could I make her want me instead?

I drank more while trying to stop the train wreck in my head. There's a reason that guys don't get in to the emotional relationship crap; it was making my brain hurt to have to think this much about something so simple.

Did I, or did I not, now want the girl for myself?

I wasn't sure…

I had wangled the sofa for me and Jenny, but it soon became clear that it was too big. We were sitting way too far apart. In the end I stretched out and lay the full length of the sofa. At least that way I was physically touching Jenny. She was sitting upright and looking really uncomfortable, but as time went by she began to slump and lean back into me more and more.

I watched her through half-closed eyes. She was sipping at her beer, and I could tell from her polite expression that she didn't like it. She was also watching Scott and Trudy out of the corner of her eye while pretending that she wasn't interested.

That's when I noticed that Scott was doing the same.

They kept catching each other's eye and then looking away. This went on for a while and then they forgot to look away.

It was sickening. I was actually watching the start of their relationship happening right in front of me.

I should have been happy for her, but instead it

really bugged me. They were doing it right under mine and Trudy's noses.

Trudy couldn't see Scott's face, because she was leaning back against him, so she missed the moment when he gave Jenny a lingering look and a shy smile. But she didn't miss Jenny biting back her own smile as she returned Scott's look.

I think Trudy twigged there was something going on, because she suddenly cut across the music and quiet conversation to ask Scott to get her something decent to drink from the kitchen downstairs.

Everyone began to shift. Scott stood up and so did Damon, so I figured it would be a good moment to get something else for Jenny as well.

Down in the kitchen, Damon suggested that Rachel might like a vodka and tonic. I plucked the glasses off the shelf and spun the lid off the tonic. Damon got ice and Scott found the vodka. I added ice to the glasses and then the tonic, but when Scott handed me the vodka I only topped up two of the glasses. Jenny wasn't a big drinker, and I thought she might find the vodka a bit much. On the other hand, maybe it was kind of parenty of me to make that decision for her. She might want to get drunk. I stood there dithering with indecision. If I was trying to score then I might have given her a drink to relax her a bit, but instead I felt like I was more her chaperone than her date. I had to decide before the boys noticed anything. I capped the vodka and put it away, then picked up the non-alcoholic drink for Jenny.

I was right. The look on Jenny's face when I told her it was a virgin drink was pure relief. She was looking at me like I was wonderful, and I really liked it. Usually only Scott got that look. I couldn't help but think that Scott would never have been aware enough of her feelings to even consider giving her a fake drink.

Clearly I had it bad. When was the last time I was this aware of a girl's likes and dislikes? I was pretty good at noticing stuff most of the time – it was an invaluable skill for getting girls – but with Jenny I actually cared.

I stretched out again, and went back to watching

her. I was taking in the little things, like the exact colour of her hair and the dusting of freckles on her nose, and the way she snapped her teeth together when she yawned, just like a cat.

I could see she was getting tired. I tried to mentally encourage her to lie down. I was willing it with all the power of the force that I could muster. I projected my thoughts at her: "Come on, Jones, lie back and snuggle up with me, you know you would be more comfortable." Obviously she was immune to telepathic suggestion. She slumped more but didn't lie down. The anticipation of waiting and hoping was getting to me.

"Why don't you stretch out, Jones, you look like a poker sat up like that. There's room enough here for both of us." I patted the sofa invitingly.

I scootched over as much as I could, making it look as though we would barely be touching. But when she did finally give in and lie down, I couldn't help turning on my side to create a more intimate position.

I wanted to put my arm around her, but I knew

she'd bolt. And the temptation to slide my leg over hers was immense, but to what end? Instead I just enjoyed having her body pressed against mine. She was lying on her back, but when I didn't try to touch her she relaxed and shifted onto her side to get more comfortable. I was practically curled around her now. Her bum was pressed against my groin and it was an absolute peach. Her hair smelled gorgeous – maybe an apple shampoo? And I loved the view of her curves, her bare waist dipping away and then the rise of her hip bone.

When I finally looked away it was to find Scott staring squarely at us. He had been watching me check out every inch of her and he seemed annoyed.

I bit back a sigh. I had to remember the purpose of our date. I seemed to be in danger of forgetting it. On the other hand, if Scott had finally worked out that Jenny liked him, and was now feeling jealous of my proximity to her, then that was a good thing for Jenny.

Jenny became aware of Scott's expression about a second after I did. I could feel her panic. I firmly pressed her into the sofa. The advantage of our position meant that I could talk straight into her ear and no one could hear me or see what I was saying.

"Don't move," I whispered, "that's exactly how you want him to look. He's finally noticing you, don't blow it now."

She nodded imperceptibly and tried to act like she hadn't noticed. After a while I felt her start to fall asleep.

I rested my hand on her hip, but she didn't move. Scott narrowed his eyes on us again. I just couldn't resist rubbing it in a little and I let my fingers trail across her bare stomach. Jenny mumbled and actually snuggled closer to me. I circled her fake tattoo, just to wind Scott up a bit.

Jenny was clearly ticklish; she was smiling and pressing her backside even closer.

Oh dear, she really needed to stop moving like that.

"Uh, Jones?" I shook her gently.

"Mmm?" she said, half asleep.

"You might want to stop wiggling your bum, or

you're going to get a shock."

I felt her whole body stiffen as she worked out what I meant.

"Don't you dare move!" I said as she was about to scramble away. "Your body is the only thing covering my dignity. The boys will laugh if you jump up *and* they will see exactly why."

"Then make it go away." She sounded mortified.

"I'm working on it." I laughed quietly and tried to think of unattractive things, like the way the Headmaster picks his nose in Friday Assembly.

But I'd woken Jenny up and I could sense she was restless now. It didn't help that Scott and Trudy were clearly building up to their night in Blake's spare room. Scott may well have properly noticed Jenny tonight, but he wasn't going to pass up his planned session of naked fun with Trudy.

"Have you had enough?" I asked Jenny. She nodded, looking tired.

We said our goodbyes and headed out. Scott's eyes followed us, but he was smart enough not to risk saying anything that might be noticed by Trudy.

Jenny was quiet as we started to walk, but I knew exactly what she was thinking. It was all there in her expressive face. She was wondering exactly what my physical reaction to her meant for our relationship.

There was no way on earth that she was ready to hear that I actually did fancy her, and she was so into Scott that she would run a mile if I said I had feelings for her as well. Much better to play the role of her friend and see how it all panned out. The chances were looking really good that she and Scott would get together. We'd come so far that it would be crazy now not to help her see it through. She would be happy with Scott, and Scott would be happy with her. And I would pretend that I was happy too.

Eventually I knew I had to broach the subject.

"You're reading too much into it, Jones. You're worrying now, aren't you? You think I'm falling for you, but you only have eyes for Scott?"

"I didn't think that!" she said, when it was obvious from her expression that I'd hit the nail right on the head.

I knew what I had to say. "You're a girl, you're pretty and you were in my arms, it's just biology. No, I don't like you that way."

I could tell that was exactly what she wanted to hear. Jenny slipped her arm through mine, pulling me close.

"You know what, Nick? I never realised how nice you were. You have an awful reputation at school as a hard-arse, but you're just a squashy marshmallow underneath aren't you?"

Hah! I felt like a marshmallow that had just been stomped on. If only she knew how close I was to being selfish and ruining the whole thing. Letting her do her own work with Scott and letting him bang Trudy for the foreseeable. But I wouldn't ruin it all now, would I?

"You're a good friend." She smiled at me.

"Lucky me," I said more sarcastically than I meant to.

She laughed. "Oh dear, this is the second Saturday

night in a row you've had to go without getting any action because of me, isn't it?"

"Yup, but as long as you appreciate it then I can live with it."

"I do." She nodded. "I'll totally make sure you get an A in Science."

"Great." Silly girl, as if I cared about that.

When we reached her house I wanted to kiss her so badly, but I managed to hold off. How had I gotten into this? I was simply helping her to get Scott to notice her, and now I was wondering if there was anyway to get her to notice *me*!

The Line

On Sunday after football we met up with Scott again at the café on the green. Scott looked seriously tired.

"Looks like someone was up all night?" Damon teased him.

"Yeah." Scott flicked his hair out of his eyes. "But not in a good way. That girl is properly mental. We were up arguing most of the night about god knows what, and then mid-fight she'd jump on me and expect me to be up and ready for it. I didn't know if I was coming or going, and I mean that literally!"

I smirked. I remembered Trudy's fondness for both rows and sex, and the combination of the two. It was definitely enough to leave a man confused. But she was a tiger in the sack when she was angry, so Scott should be looking a bit happier.

But Scott didn't look happy. He'd probably not been able to get it up under that kind of pressure. Then again, Trudy had been wearing a corset under her t-shirt last night – I'd recognised the straps showing – and Trudy in a corset was a sight that surely no red-blooded male would be able to resist.

"So did you come or did you go?" Spudhead asked.

Scott sighed. "In the end I got out of there. I don't date possessive girls. I had enough of that from Stacey, always asking where I was and who I was with."

Interesting. I would hazard a guess that their argument was in fact about Jenny. Trudy had sussed Scott's interest in sweet Jenny Jones and she wasn't at all happy about it. And clearly Scott hadn't denied it vehemently enough, or been smitten enough with Trudy's assets, to forget himself and just take the verbal battering, along with all the other goods on offer.

"So it's over? You've broken up?" I clarified. Scott nodded firmly. I felt kind of gut-punched that it had happened so quickly. I thought I'd have more time and more fake dates with Jenny, but I supposed this was good news. I knew Jenny would be ecstatic to hear it, anyway.

Almost like he could hear my thoughts, Scott said, "I need someone calmer, someone nice, like you have with Jenny."

Ow, the knife just twisted a bit, but Scott was unaware. I tried not to sound bitter as I replied, "We're not really dating, she's just a friend."

Damon raised his eyebrows, "A pretty good friend if you ask me; you were all over her on the sofa last night."

I grinned. "Well, a man's got to try! What would you do if you had a beautiful girl in your arms? Lie there like a lemon? Or see if you could cop a feel?"

"So what did you manage to feel?" Damon smiled back.

I waggled my own eyebrows in a *wouldn't you like to know* kind of way, but said nothing more. I'd done my good deed and I wasn't feeling very charitable about it.

In science on Monday, Jenny was full of the joys just because Scott had waved at her in registration. She was lit up inside like a candle in a paper lantern, and after my news I was sure she would just about float away.

"Scott broke up with Trudy yesterday," I told her.

Yup, the girl was in raptures.

"I'm completely thrilled. I totally love you!" she said, not realising the words made my pulse jump.

"I take it you mean that you love me in a platonic *what a good friend* kind of way?" I found myself wishing that she had said it for real; was there the slightest chance she felt anything more than friendship for me?

"Well, duh, obviously. But I really do. You're amazing, I can't believe you've done all this for me."

No, clearly I was permanently relegated to friend status.

"Who says I did this for you? Maybe I did it for Scott? And I'm not admitting to having done anything at all." I couldn't help my tone being a bit sulky.

Jenny patted my hand in what I supposed was meant to be a reassuring manner, but was actually rather crushing to my poor heart.

"I know you did. I'm not totally naïve," she said

kindly

"Yes you are, Jennifer Jones, yes you are," I said, keeping my eyes on my books so she wouldn't see how gutted I was feeling suddenly.

I spent the next couple of days avoiding her completely. I was just so unsure of my feelings, and I needed some perspective. I was suddenly in a love triangle, except that nobody actually loved me. More of a love *line* really, from me to Jenny to Scott. Except that I was sure Scott liked her back, so basically I was the odd man out.

Why was I suddenly torturing myself over this girl? Was it because I couldn't have her? Was I that shallow? I didn't think I was. And it wasn't even as if she was that much of a stunner. I know I'd called her beautiful in front of the boys, but the truth was her looks were only slightly better than average. And yet, the more I looked at her, the more beautiful she seemed to become. Was that what they meant about beauty being in the eye of the beholder? That when you really stopped to look, you saw the beauty? I wondered if Scott had noticed that Jenny's eyes were the same green-grey as the river on a cloudy day? Or that when the sun shone on her hair it went from brown-blonde to a rich gold?

Somewhere I had crossed a line between liking her and really liking her. But she was on the other side of that line and I didn't know how to make her cross it. Also I wanted her to do it all of her own accord; I didn't want to manipulate her into liking me. Why didn't she notice me the way she always noticed Scott?

By Wednesday I'd made my mind up. I needed to get Scott and Jenny together fast and then I needed to go and get a life. A new girlfriend. If I got them together on Friday, then I could hit that club on Baker Street on Saturday and meet someone. Probably not a long-term kind of girl – after all, some of the birds in that place were ropey as heck – but at least a bit of solace, the wooden-spoon prize for the loser. And just maybe, things wouldn't work out with Jenny and Scott, and in time, when the dust had settled, perhaps I could try again with her. Though knowing my recent luck, they would probably end up married...

I worked out a scenario that would force Scott to go to Jenny's defence, which would make him feel like a hero and should make me the villain who obviously doesn't get the girl. It would have worked best of all if I hadn't told Jenny the plan, because then her reactions would have been totally real; but I couldn't bear for her to think badly of me. So in the end I told her that the two of us would have a public row and that I would be nasty to her. She should then leave and Scott should go after her. I could see she wasn't at all sure about it, but I didn't mention the fact that I would also be blaming her for liking Scott instead of me. It was nothing less than the truth, and so I knew I would be convincing; but I couldn't imagine Jenny agreeing in advance to that kind of humiliation for both of us, so I kept my mouth shut on the finer details of the plan.

Friday evening almost went like clockwork. Scott

was giving Jenny plenty of attention, and my feelings were genuine when I showed a rather unattractive possessive streak. I staged the argument with Jenny, she got upset and left.

I'd embarrassed Scott too, but I could see he was mostly angry with me for hurting Jenny's feelings. He called me a pathetic arsehole, and asked what the hell my problem was. After all, I had made a point of saying we were just friends so why was I being such a tosser to Jenny? He was properly winding himself up, which I hadn't expected. So I cut in on his rant.

"If you feel so strongly, then why are you here shouting at me? Go after her, you muppet." I couldn't help but smile at the confusion on his face.

Scott and I had been close friends for years – most of our lives, in fact – and he knew me pretty well, so it shouldn't have surprised me that Scott finally cottoned on that maybe I was setting them up.

I watched the realisation dawning on his face as he continued to gape at me. I watched as he twigged that I was up to something, then laughed as his brain began working it all out.

I'd planned to keep Scott in the dark about what a manipulative sod I'd been, but actually I would much rather he knew it and didn't instead think that I was deliberately hurting Jenny.

"So you and Jenny really are just friends?"

"Yes! Look buddy, she's liked you for ages and you were too dumb to see what a gem she was, so I thought I'd help out a bit."

Scott nodded, accepting the truth in what I was saying. Eventually he put his hand on my shoulder. "You're a good friend."

I resisted the urge to swear. I'd heard that phrase far too much already from Jenny. I tried not to sound sarky as I said, "Yeah, I know."

"And you really don't want her for yourself?" Scott looked like he really couldn't believe that. I guess my true feelings had been showing through a little more than I thought.

I couldn't look him in the eye as I avoided giving him a direct answer. "It wouldn't matter if I did. She likes *you*."

Scott paused again. Damn, that was the problem with trying to fool a friend who knew you so well.

"Go, Scott. She'll be halfway home by now," I urged him.

He looked at me for just a moment longer, indecision in his eyes as he tried to gauge how much I wasn't saying, but then his instinct to follow Jenny won out and he went after her.

I felt instantly deflated. Scott was a good guy and he would never take a girl that he knew I really liked, so I had obviously managed to hide the true depths of my feelings for her.

Now all that remained was to get rip-roaring drunk and toast the happy couple...

Stupid Is...

I sat down to find Damon and Rachel both staring at me. I gave a half smile and a shrug of embarrassment that they had just witnessed it all, but what was done was done.

Damon slowly shook his head. "Man, you really do have shit for brains sometimes."

"What do you mean?" I asked, fishing two bottles of beer out of the cooler, both for me.

"Have you actually told the girl that you like her?"

I closed my eyes. Other than Scott, Damon would be the only other person that knew exactly what I was feeling without me having to say it.

"There wasn't any point," I mumbled; "she made it pretty clear how she felt."

"Maybe she didn't know how she was truly feeling?" Rachel suggested.

"Look, she likes Scott. They'd be good together," I snapped.

Damon frowned at me. "Scott will meet a nice girl

anyway. You, on the other hand, have god-awful taste in girls. She was good for *you*."

"What is this? The Jenny Jones fan club? You've barely spoken to her for years and now you're acting like you know her and what she may or may not be feeling?" I downed the second beer.

"No. I do know you, though, and what you're feeling," Damon pushed the point.

"Can we just drop it?" I glared at him.

"I was just saying…"

"Well, don't. Let's just get plastered and have some fun, okay?"

Damon nodded. He wasn't exactly experienced at talking about emotional crap, but since he and Rachel had hooked up, I could see he was in that happy place where he wanted us all to be happy too.

The subject was changed, but I couldn't stop my thoughts from constantly returning to Jenny.

Why was I so pissed off? I'd made my choice earlier in the week. I had decided not to pursue Jennifer Jones and to help her and Scott get together, and I had been so sure it was the right decision.

Jenny had approached me to help her, and I had done my part. What happened now was up to the two of them.

Had she noticed me at all during our recent time together? I had certainly begun to notice her far more than ever before. And didn't she deserve to know all the facts before she made her decision? She should know that I liked her... More than liked her. Her feelings for Scott might not even be real, just a crush that had developed into a bit of an obsession.

Friends came and went and the sky got darker. I stared moodily at my beer. How many had I had? I couldn't remember.

What was Jenny doing now? Had she and Scott decided to jump right into a relationship? Maybe they were all over each other at this very moment. Rolling around on the grass on the green, or up against the cricket hut.

Dammit, I should have kissed her first. Shown her how things could be between us. She wouldn't think of me just as a friend if we shared the kind of kiss I was imagining. Of course, she might just slap my face if I actually tried it. Or she might not…

Around eleven p.m. I ran out of booze. The evening was still warm but people were packing up and heading off to parties or home.

Damon and Rachel had gone, and Spudhead was asleep on my picnic rug. I got unsteadily to my feet. Normally I would be suggesting we hit a club, but I was drunk and I just wanted to go home and mope.

No, I wanted to go and see if Jenny was at home. Just go past her house and check if her light was on.

I left Spudhead and my rug in the dubious care of Paul, and disappeared into the night.

The walk to Jenny's cleared my head a bit. I would just make sure she was at home and then I'd leave. It would be mental to do anything else.

I knew which was her window, because when I'd walked her home last week, I'd waited until she was safely inside and then I had seen her bedroom light come on a minute later.

But as I stood outside her house I had no idea if she was there or not. The whole place was in darkness. So she was either still out with Scott or she was in bed already.

I picked up a handful of small stones and judged the distance to her window.

The sensible thing to do was to leave. After all, if she was with Scott then I didn't really want to know, plus I didn't want to accidentally wake her parents; and if she was in bed then she might be annoyed that I'd woken her up, especially as I had no good reason for doing so.

Sensible was for sober people. I chucked the stones and was rewarded with a rattle as they hit her window.

She was there! Her window opened straight away.

"Who's that?" she whispered.

"It's me, Nick."

"Hang on, I'll be right down."

I couldn't stop smiling as I wandered over to her garden swing and sat down to wait. How had I ever been unsure about my feelings for this girl? I was so happy that she was home and not with Scott. I felt all light-headed about seeing her again, even though it had literally only been three hours.

Jenny ran across the grass and threw her arms around me.

"You did it! Thank you so much! Did Scott come back to the river afterwards? He asked me out!"

As I put my arms around her in return I could feel every curve of her body through the thin t-shirt material. I teased her about the fact that I could tell she didn't have a bra on, and then instantly wished I'd kept my mouth shut as she pulled away from me. Her t-shirt came down to just above the knee, and from here I couldn't even tell if she was wearing anything at all underneath it. I assumed she must have some kind of bottoms on, as Jenny certainly wasn't brave enough to go without. No, she would be wearing some cute boy-shorts or something like that. I looked at the t-shirt in bemusement; was that Frodo staring back at me?

Jenny crossed her arms defensively over her breasts.

"Don't wind me up," she chided. "Right now I freaking adore you. You are without doubt the smartest male in the whole world. And you got me Scott! You didn't just make him notice me, he's asked me out! To dinner at La Reine tomorrow night. What can I do to thank you? If there is anything at all I can do for you in return, just name it."

"La Reine?" Oh, bloody hell, he really liked her; what was I doing? But I had to tell her how I felt. She had a right to know. I just wasn't sure if I could say the words. I swung back and forth, contemplating what on earth to say. The trouble was that my usually silver tongue was guided by my brain, and my brain wasn't working. All I wanted to do was to take her in my arms again, feel her body against mine. I wanted to kiss her. Then she would know how much I wanted her. Then she would know how good we could be together. But if Scott had also kissed her tonight then it would be all kinds of wrong. I wavered back and forth, wondering what to say and what to do. Maybe I should just go home and stop bothering her. But then

I would never know; and just maybe if she knew how I felt, it might make a difference?

"Did he kiss you?" I eventually asked.

"No, but he kissed my hand."

"Oh, bleh!" I couldn't help but scoff, "That's a bit cheesy, isn't it?" Wasn't that what Greek waiters did? Not a guy who likes you and wants to show you exactly how much!

I pulled her closer. "I'm glad he didn't kiss you properly," I said, making up my mind. "I wanted to be first."

"Huh?" She looked totally confused.

"I want you to kiss me," I clarified.

"What? Why?"

Oh no, she was backing away. I tightened my grip on her t-shirt, yanking her even closer. I *had* to kiss her. If she rejected me then fine, I had my answer; but first I needed to show her how I felt about her.

"Because you said you would do something for me in return. Because I've not kissed a girl in two weeks, dancing attendance on you. Because it's late and I've been drinking and I want you to. It's how I want you to thank me." I said the first thing that came into my head, even though I knew it was a low blow, but I couldn't think of how else to make her do it.

"Don't you think it's a bad idea? I mean, what would Scott think if I say yes to going out with him and then made out with you? Talk about sending mixed messages! I can't play games and not care like you can."

I could see the indecision in her eyes. She just needed a little push. She *wanted* me to make her I was sure of it, even if it was just curiosity on her part.

"You said you would do anything I wanted in return for my help. *Just name it*," I mimicked her. "All I want is for you to kiss me, just once, like you mean it. I'm not going to tell Scott. He'll never know." God, I hoped I was right about her feelings, otherwise I was being a total pig. What if the alcohol was clouding my judgement?

"But why?" Even as she asked me, she swayed slightly towards me; she was already moving in for the kiss. I felt my lip curl into a smile, as I knew for sure that she truly did want it.

"Shut up and kiss me, Jones." I grabbed her peachy bum and dragged her against me. She looked startled but didn't pull away. So I kissed her.

Her reaction totally threw me. After a moment of hesitation she practically took over! Sweet Jenny Jones had a lusty streak. She kissed the crap out of me. One minute I was trying to persuade her to kiss me, and then next she was crawling on to my lap with her arms around my neck. It was the most amazing kiss ever, like she really wanted me too and we were meeting on a totally new level.

I ran my hands down her back and under her t-shirt. I couldn't help myself, I had to touch her. I tried to keep my hands low but the temptation was too much and one slid upwards, cupping a perfect breast. Instead of slapping me, she moaned and wrapped her legs around me.

I was getting dizzy with desire. I wanted to lay her down on the grass and peel off her t-shirt, and kiss her everywhere.

Oh crapoly, what was I doing? I had to stop this now or it wouldn't stop at all!

"Whoa, Jen." It took an almost inhuman amount of effort, but I broke the kiss and pulled back.

She looked even more amazed than I was. Her eyes were glazed and for a moment I wondered if she had been drinking after she'd left earlier, but I knew that wasn't it. She might not be in love with me, but she sure as hellfire desired me. And judging by the look on her face, she hadn't ever even realised it.

She actually pouted as I moved out of reach, which was so adorably cute that I almost went straight back for more. Instead I lifted her and slid out from under her, putting in as much physical distance as I could bear. It was torture, but I had to stop. I couldn't believe I had done it at all. What had I been thinking? Now I was consumed with wanting her for my own and she was probably completely confused, and none of it was fair on Scott.

"Sorry," she said, making me feel like an even

bigger jerk than ever.

"No, *I'm* sorry, Jen. That was totally out of order of me. It's one thing to kiss you, but I think even Scott would be pretty unforgiving if I shagged his new girlfriend the night before your first date."

"I wasn't going to do that!" She looked horrified.

"Hah, could have fooled me, Jones, seems like you wanted it to me." I didn't mean to be nasty, but I needed to put some emotional distance between us. If she was any sweeter I'd be down on my knees begging her to love me.

She just looked at the floor, so I had no idea what she was thinking.

"I'd better go." I reached out and touched her shoulder, wanting to see the look on her face.

It was a look that slayed me, she wanted me to kiss her again! I just knew it; but that path was too dangerous now. I had to get away before I did something I really regretted and she ended up hating me.

She had to work out for herself what she wanted.

At least now she knew how I felt.

"Have a good time tomorrow. We'll talk more next week, okay?" I felt sick at the thought of her going on her date with Scott, but it wasn't my call anymore. I'd done what I'd come to do, and then some. It was definitely time to go.

I walked away feeling worse than ever, but sure that she might finally have noticed me.

Part 3 – Jenny

Stella Wilkinson

The Date

When I woke up on Saturday morning I was totally confused. Scott liked me – yay. But now it seemed Nick liked me? I'd had no idea. But he must do, otherwise why come over last night? He must have a phone book full of girls he could ring for a booty call, yet he came to see me. He'd kissed me, and what a kiss! But then he'd been the one to stop it as well. If he really liked me then why had he stopped it? Another good question was why hadn't *I* stopped it?

I'd just woken up from a whole night of dreaming about Nick. The way he looked all dressed in black, the way he teased me in science class, the way he kissed me...

Why hadn't I spent the night dreaming about my date with Scott? After all, I'd been working up to this date for weeks, months even!

Had I really gone from having no one interested in me at all to having two boys?

Or maybe I hadn't at all. Scott might not be particularly into me; after all, he was dating someone else last week. But then why ask me for dinner? And Nick might have just been drunk; and like he said, I kind of owed him a kiss. But I couldn't imagine Nick acting that way unless he actually liked me.

So... Scott or Nick?

Scott was funny, handsome, kind, athletic, perfect.

Nick – Hmm. Never serious, a bit of a womaniser, hardly boyfriend material!

I nodded to myself. Why was I even thinking about it? Nothing had changed, it was just a kiss. A meaningless, amazing, kiss...

It was Scott. It had always been Scott.

I spent the day in town with Andrea shopping for new earrings and a hair clip and looking at shoes I couldn't afford. I found myself staring at a shop window, where a pair of blue shoes sat next to a pair of red shoes. Two totally different shoes, but I liked both.

I told Andi all about my fake fight with Nick, and

about Scott coming after me. But I didn't tell her about Nick. I don't know why, but I just wasn't ready to share it, like it was a secret personal moment between him and me.

Andrea was over the moon for me that I might get together with Scott, and finally confessed that she had feelings for Bradley. We got a bit over-excited about how our lives were changing for the better.

"Come further up, come further in!" I quoted C.S. Lewis, feeling like we were entering a brave new world. One that included cool boyfriends.

I spent an hour in the bath, then dressed with great care. I wanted Scott to like the real me, so I ditched sexy and went with a pretty white shirt, a peasant skirt and sandals.

My dad dropped me into town and my insides were total butterflies all the way. I had a massive fit of nerves as I stood outside La Reine, but there was Scott in the window, inside at a lovely table. He looked up and smiled and waved.

It was finally happening. The date I had dreamed

about for so long.

Scott stood to meet me and kissed me on the cheek. "You look lovely," he said.

"You too," I smiled. He really did look good. A designer rugby shirt over jeans, but somehow he looked smart. He also smelled great, of something fresh, clean and citrusy.

I had this horrible twinge of guilt in my stomach though. How could I have been so stupid as to kiss Nick last night? I wondered if I should tell Scott. Get it all out in the open. But I didn't want to be the cause of any friction in their friendship. I just desperately wished I hadn't done it, because now the memory of it was somehow tainting my date.

We ordered pizza, and Scott asked if I would like wine. I was going to say no, but then I thought that maybe it would help settle me, so I got a glass of white, but a glass of water as well to balance it out.

I tried to enjoy the pleasure of his company. It wasn't difficult; Scott was so funny and so nice to be around. He was easy to talk to, and soon we were joking and laughing across the table to each other.

About two-thirds of the way through the meal I paused, my fork halfway to my mouth, as I got a sudden sense of someone watching me. I looked around but I couldn't see anyone. I looked out the window. There were lots of passing crowds, mainly young people off to Baker Street, where the bars and clubs were. I couldn't see anyone I knew. I tried to shake off the feeling, but the feeling persisted and it felt like Nick. I decided it was my conscience.

After pizza, Scott insisted we have a dessert. I said I only would if he let me pay for half the meal, but he wouldn't hear of it. In the end I gave in and we shared a Tiramisu. It was one of the most exciting moments of my life, both of us digging our spoons into the same dessert and licking the chocolate off them. My conscience stopped bothering me, and I was happy.

When we left the restaurant Scott took my hand. I twined my fingers through his and we walked down the street together in a blissful daze.

We walked past the town hall, where a fountain

sprayed different-coloured water as the lights set inside the fountain changed from blue to green to yellow to pink. It was a perfect romantic spot, and I giggled as Scott gently pushed me up against one of the columns round the grand entrance to the building.

"Is this okay?" He gave me an almost shy smile.

I nodded, almost too excited to speak.

Then he kissed me.

I waited for the bone melting, the brain mush and the jelly knees that I had experienced with Nick, and I got nothing...

It was very nice, but no fireworks.

Oh crap! I'd made the wrong choice. I'd thought I was in love with Scott, but somewhere along the way it had changed to Nick!

I pulled away, looking at him with wide eyes. How on earth was I going to explain?

"What is it?" His hand cupped my face.

"I'm sorry," I stammered, then didn't know what to say next. How could I say that last night I had been kissing Nick and that it had felt like much more? I would sound like a total tart.

Scott stepped back. "It's Nick, isn't it?"

He didn't look mad; in fact he looked almost pleased as I nodded.

"I'm so sorry," I said again, "I know it sounds dumb, but I only just realised... Please let me pay you back for dinner."

"Don't be daft." Scott smiled at me. "I had a very nice dinner with a pretty girl, who just happens to be in love with my best friend. And if I'm not mistaken, then he rather likes her back."

"Do you think so?" I winced as my voice came out sounding almost desperate. "I mean, I know he likes me, but I don't think he likes me like that."

"Believe me, he does. I should have noticed it straight away." Scott looked thoughtful, as though he was remembering something that happened. "I just hope he's not going to be an idiot about it now."

I looked at my watch – it was nearly ten o'clock. Nick was probably already kissing someone else.

"You know, I seem to remember Damon saying they were all going to Dragon, that new club on Baker Street tonight. It has massive queues, so they probably aren't even inside yet. It's only a couple of streets away, do you fancy walking over there?"

"You don't mind?" I looked up at him, hoping he wasn't secretly annoyed and just pretending to be incredibly nice.

He took my hand again. "Not at all; after all, it looks like my date has been cut short, so I could get into a club vibe instead. Have a few drinks, chat up a few girls..." He grinned at me and I grinned back in relief.

We walked over to Baker Street, and as Scott said, there was a massively long queue at Dragon. Near the front we found Damon, Rachel and some others I didn't really know.

"Hey," Damon said, pulling us into the queue with them. "How was dinner?"

I felt myself blush, but Scott was casual. "Yeah, great, thanks. Where's Nick?"

Some boy, who I didn't know, said, "He went home, said he wasn't in the mood. I think he's really bummed out about this chick he likes, who…"

"Shut up, Spud!" Rachel stamped hard on his foot and the boy was silenced. He stared at Rachel with a look of hurt surprise on his face.

"I'm sorry." Rachel turned to me. "Spudhead is a bit tactless."

"Oh!" Spudhead caught up on who I was.

"It's okay," Scott told them. "She's not with me."

Damon looked down at Scott's hand, which was still holding one of mine, and raised his eyebrows. "Am I the only one who's confused?"

Scott and I dropped hands like they were hot potatoes.

"Jenny, why don't you ring Nick?" Scott suggested.

"What? No way. I just can't. I'm sorry, but I'm really not in the clubbing mood. I'm just going to go home."

Scott nodded. "Okay, do you want me to walk you?"

"Of course not." I smiled, remembering the last time he walked me home; it seemed so long ago suddenly. "I'll just get a taxi."

Baker Street was filled with taxis picking up people coming out of the many bars that lined the street, so I had no trouble flagging one down straight away.

I paused to give Scott a peck on the cheek. "Thank you so much for understanding, and for dinner, of course."

I gave the driver my address and slumped back in my seat. I knew it was silly not to ring Nick, but I had no idea what to say. How could I tell him that I had kissed Scott and that it wasn't the same?

I put my head in my hands. How had I gone from no boyfriend to almost having a choice of two but mucking it up with both of them? Nick had kissed me and then I'd blithely gone on a date with Scott. Nick probably hated me now, and even if he didn't, then he'd never actually said he liked me as anything more than a friend. In fact, when I did properly kiss him he pulled away. I was doomed to end up alone…

I'd been in my room for about half an hour, reading with the light on, when I heard the rattle against my window.

Nick!

I ran down to the front door, and putting it on the latch I slipped out into the garden.

"Oh yum, you're wearing my favourite t-shirt again," Nick said in his usual joking manner, as he swung back and forth on my swing.

"What are you doing here?" I asked, ignoring the dig at my LOTR top.

He held up his phone. "I got a cryptic text from Scott." He pushed a button to bring up the text. "He says, *It's not me, it's you.* Now what do you think he means by that?"

I blushed and looked at the floor. "I don't know," I hedged. I didn't want to have to say it.

"I saw you in the restaurant, the two of you were having a great time. So why are you home already?" Nick wasn't giving anything away either. Were we going to get stuck in a stalemate? I was too embarrassed to tell him what happened, and clearly he had no idea how I was feeling because I'd only ever talked about Scott.

I took a deep breath. "I think he means that I don't like him after all, and that I might like you instead…"

Nick stopped swinging. "And is he right?" he asked in a low voice.

"Yes," I mumbled.

Nick literally swept me off my feet.

As he lowered me gently to the grass I finally shyly looked him in the eye.

"We're a pair of idiots," he said, "I'm just glad I finally noticed you, right under my nose all this time, and you *finally* noticed me too," he gave me a fond smile. Then he kissed me again and I couldn't think about anything or anyone but him for a long long time.

The End

Books by Stella Wilkinson

The Flirting Games (Book One)
More Flirting Games (Book Two)
Further Flirting Games (Book Three)
The Flirting Games Trilogy, (Books 1 - 3)
Good @ Games (Book Four)
Flirting with Friends (Book Five)
Best Frenemies (Book Six)
Boy Girl Games (Book Seven)
A Compass Court Christmas (Book Eight)
Magic & Mayhem (Books 1 - 3)
Halloween Magic & Mayhem (Book One)
Werewolf Magic & Mayhem (Book Two)
Solstice Magic & Mayhem (Book Three)
Demon Magic & Mayhem (Book Four)
Notice Me
Remind Me
A Christmas Gift
The Fake Valentine
A Summer Thing
All Hallows Eve
Four Seasons of Romance

Find out more about the author including upcoming releases at: www.stellawilkinson.com

Keep Reading for an excerpt from Book Two in the Blue River Boys series: Remind Me

Stella Wilkinson

Remind Me
Chapter One

I stared at the back of Bradley's head in English class and cursed myself for not being smart enough as a kid to see that one day he was going to be totally hot. Not that I'm wholly to blame, his nickname "Fat Brad" was well earned. He was the short tubby kid in our class since we were in pre-school, and he stayed that way until we all hit puberty. That's when Bradley had a growth spurt, and all that weight he'd been carrying redistributed itself to all the right places.

His boy boobs reshaped into perfect pecs, his flabby frame filled out to wide shoulders, a square jaw and washboard abs, and his chunky little hands suddenly became strong and capable. I think his hands were my favourite part of him now. I watched him rolling his pen through his fingers as he listened to the teacher and I admired his skill and dexterity as the pen weaved seamlessly back and forth.

Is that sad or what? To be ridiculously impressed by him handling a pen? I probably need therapy. But the worst of it is that he could have been mine and I never followed up on it.

He'd liked me and I'd hadn't appreciated him. More fool me. Of course, we were only kids at the time. But now I had my comeuppance. These days he's a hot jock and I'm a nobody. Darn it!

"What are you thinking about?" Jenny nudged me in the ribs, her voice a low whisper.

"Huh? Nothing," I quickly looked down at my text book. "Why?"

"You've got a weird look on your face, like you're in pain but enjoying it."

Yup, that probably summed up my feelings, but I gave her a blank stare as though she was the one being weird not me.

"*No one* enjoys listening to Mr. Scanlon reading The Iliad."

"Somehow I don't think that's where your mind was," Jenny grinned, and I blushed even though she couldn't possibly know.

Mr. Scanlon flicked his eyes briefly from the book to us, and we instantly fell silent and tried to look attentive. He's scary. But my thoughts lingered on Fat Brad, or just Brad I guess. Buff Brad? Brad the babe magnet? Bradley the boy I had blown it with? Gah.

We took the long way to lunch, careful to skirt closely to the popular table of guys who ate at the picnic area outside from the moment the spring rain stopped.

Jenny has recently developed a humungous crush on Scott Lawes and was trying every trick she could think of to come to his attention. Personally I didn't think she had much chance, Scott moves in a different circle of friends and she has no classes with him except History, and we always sit with our own girly group. Scott is a guy's guy. He surrounds himself with the sporty types. Damon, Nick, Paul, Tobias, Bradley… Yeah, they're all hot, and I had no issue at all with walking out of my way to eat them up with my eyes before I ate lunch.

Jenny isn't really like that, she's had one boyfriend, and now her unrequited crush on Scott. But me? I love the smell of beefcake in the morning, or at any time really, and these boys smelled *good*.

And I don't do so badly in the romance stakes, I date, but I get bored easily with the guys in my league. I hate to say it, but mostly I only get asked out by the weedy types. Not that I have anything against them, some are cute, but nothing I can get enthusiastic about or drool over. Hence the ridiculous daydreaming over Brad the Bod.

I *really* needed to come up with a better nickname in my head if he was going to continue to invade my thoughts.

Jenny was quiet through lunch and I could see she was working up to something.

"What on your mind?" I said, after watching her push cheesecake around her plate for five minutes.

"I have a plan to make Scott Lawes notice me, but I need your help."

"Why do I get the feeling I'm not going to like this?" I grimaced at her, teasing slightly because she was taking it all so seriously.

"Please, Andi. You know I'd do it for you." She gave me a beseeching look.

"What exactly would you do for me?" I said, suspiciously

She took a deep breath. "Well... The problem, as I see it, is that as far as Scott is concerned I don't really exist."

I nodded cautiously, encouraging her to continue.

"So basically he needs to see a lot more of me."

"Let me guess – you're planning to take up sports?" I grinned, because it was so unlikely.

"Don't laugh," she chided. "This is important to me. But no, nothing as dramatic as that! I've written a list of things he does, places he goes, and who his friends are." She actually pulled out a notepad and a pen.

"So you're planning on stalking him?" I laughed some more and she glared at me.

"Uh, yes, actually. I want to be everywhere he is until he realizes what a lot we have in common, and that's kind of where you come in."

"Uh oh." I mimed a psycho knife attack. "What exactly am I supposed to do? Follow him around with a walkie-talkie feeding back his movements when you're not there?"

"Even better." She gave me a big smile. "You're going to date Fat Brad and he's going to tell you."

I literally choked on my drink. I'd just been daydreaming about Bradley and now she blithely announces I'm going to date him? Just like that, as if it were easy. I mean, I would do almost anything for my best friend, but walk up to Bradley and tell him we're suddenly a couple? Yeah, right! I kept spluttering as I imagined the humiliation.

"I'm going to what?" she squeaked, finally.

"Listen," she jabbing my pen in my direction, "Scott goes out with his friends a lot, right? And we don't get invited because we're not in his group. So how do we get into his group? One of us has to get chummy with one of his friends." She smiled happily, as if it were simple.

"No way! Not on your life, Jen. When have I ever asked you to do anything like that for me?"

"Hmm, how about the time you threw up on the back of Danny Cannon's head on the school bus and I pretended it was me because you had a crush on him? Or the time you sat in dog crap and I gave you my skirt and wore my gym kit for a whole day because you were supposed to be meeting Brandon Snider for lunch? Or…"

"Okay, okay, I owe you! But *Fat Brad?*"

"I know," she sighed, "but he's the obvious choice. He's liked you since we were about five years old, and he isn't actually fat any more, is he? He lost all that weight last year; it's just a nickname now. And he's not *bad*-looking. I'm not suggesting you actually have to date him, but maybe you could flirt with him a bit? Give off the impression that you *might* be interested, if

only you hung out more? Then perhaps casually ask
what he's up to for the weekend or where they might
all be going?"

I thought about that for a moment. Bradley *had*
liked me once upon a time, but that time was in the
long distant past. Was it possible he might still have
some residual feelings for me? Could I somehow
remind him that he'd once fancied me and I hadn't
changed. Hmm, probably not. The fact was that *I*
might still be much the same, but he wasn't. *He'd*
changed, and why would the new version of him still
be into same old me?

Me, that isn't exactly a stunner. I mean, I don't
think I'm a troll, but when I look in the mirror I'm not
all that happy. I think my nose is too wide, and no
matter how much I pay to get my eyebrows threaded,
they are still kind of wonky. And while Bradley got
more handsome, I got some spots on my chin, and
hair that kinks if I don't blow dry it for at least half an
hour. Which means that while he might have liked me

before, he could now be aiming a little higher up the food chain in looks.

On the other hand, Jenny wasn't asking a lot. It sounded scary but actually she was just asking me to flirt with him. I could do that, couldn't I? Hadn't I wanted to anyway? I just needed to work up the nerve.

Jenny had done lots of things that made her look stupid just to help me out, so I could totally do this for her. But I still felt terrified that he might coldly reject my advances, or worse he might laugh, and everyone else would laugh too.

I looked at Jenny's pleading face and rolled my eyes in acceptance. "Fine, but if I do this, we are *so* even, got it?"

She hugged me, then we both looked up as Bradley walked past.

My stomach dropped to my knees, and my palms began to sweat, but I stood up resolutely. "I've got a Geography lesson with him right now."

"Go, girl. Take one for the team," she encouraged.

"Fine. But *the team* owes me an ice cream after school!"

Available now on Amazon

Notice Me

Made in the USA
Middletown, DE
24 March 2018